GARBAGE
ISLAND

THE NEARLY ALWAYS PERILOUS ADVENTURES
OF ARCHIBALD SHREW

GARBAGE ISLAND

FRED
KOEHLER

BOYDS MILLS PRESS
AN IMPRINT OF HIGHLIGHTS
Honesdale, Pennsylvania

Boyds Mills Press
An Imprint of Highlights
815 Church Street
Honesdale, Pennsylvania 18431
boydsmillspress.com
Printed in the United States of America

ISBN: 978-1-62979-675-8 (hc) • 978-1-68437-376-5 (pb) • 978-1-62979-141-9 (eBook)

Library of Congress Control Number: 2018940032

First edition
10 9 8 7 6 5 4 3 2 1

Design by Barbara Grzeslo
The text is set in Apollo.
The titles are set in CrustiWacky.
The illustrations are done in digital media.

For Duane,

whom I threatened to write into a book

if he didn't behave himself

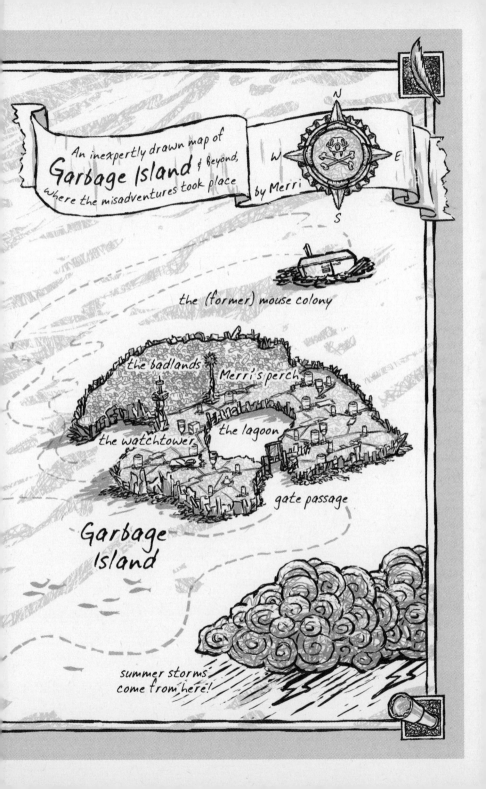

Chapter 1

Mr. Popli looked out from his only porthole into the world, scrunched his whiskers, and gasped.

What stole his breath was not seeing Archibald Shrew in the lagoon, but rather the ramshackle floating bicycle that he appeared to be pedaling. Nearly the size of Mr. Popli's houseboat, the sea-cycle carved through the water like a tuna. "Popli! Look at me!" Archie called as he zipped within a tail's length of the mouse, spraying salt water through the open porthole and rocking the houseboat no small amount.

"ARCHIBALD!" Mr. Popli bellowed, half in fury at the soaking and half in wonder at Archie's latest invention. A pair of plastic bottles, poked through with Popsicle sticks and tongue depressors like paddle wheels, spun in the water. A belt system of string and rubber bands ran between the wheels and a framework of plastic tubing and irrigation pipe. A genuine coil spring created the propulsion for the entire mechanism.

As the shrew pedaled, the large spring wound tighter. When he lifted his feet, the sea-cycle shot off so quickly Archie could only manage to cling to the steering mechanism, if in fact he could steer at all.

"My name is ARCHIEEEEEEE!" cried the shrew, flying past a second time and drenching Mr. Popli again.

A name I wish I'd never heard! thought Mr. Popli, scrambling out through his porthole. But before he could say anything, the sea-cycle careened into a half-sunken Styrofoam cooler. Archie shot into the air, somersaulted over the protective wall that held together their garbage island, and vanished into the hungry arms of the sea.

"Overboard!" Mr. Popli yelled, as he bounded to a twisted antenna atop a weathered citrus crate to look for signs of Archie. "OVERBOARD! Sound the bell!" The islanders had worked hard to build a secure place to live, and for all his fumbling, Archie was a part of their community. But he'd just gone rocketing beyond the only safety they knew.

A bell rang in the distance. Insects, reptiles, and mammals emerged from their homes, answering the call. Many poured into the water in makeshift rowboats and tiny skiffs. One small yellowish bird chirruped from above the gate leading out to the ocean. "Here! Here! He's this way!"

The boats rowed across the lagoon toward the circling bird, creatures heaving oars against the ocean. Scrambling from the citrus crate to the wall itself, Mr. Popli called out orders. "Angus! It's quicker to your left! Janice! Go around that part of the lagoon—there's barbed wire below the surface! Sven! That canal is blocked! You'll have to double back!"

"Hurry!" chirped the bird. "He's drowning!" Mr. Popli narrowed his eyes, but could only see a vague shape. The silhouette vanished and reappeared as the shrew struggled against the waves.

"Snakespit," Mr. Popli cursed. "Merri, can you get to one of the skiffs? He needs a float, and quickly!"

"Yes, sir!" The bird flitted down to the nearest vessel to retrieve a Styrofoam float wrapped in thread. By now all of the families nearby had gathered along the wall to watch the attempted rescue. A pair of yellow-and-black lizards grunted as they turned the handle of a fishing reel nailed to a board at the top of the wall. The reel retracted a heavy braided line that inched up a tall panel from the depths. As soon as this gate cleared the waterline, boats swept from the lagoon into the open ocean.

"He's got the float!" warbled Merri. "And the skiffs are closing in!"

Mr. Popli slid down from the wall and collapsed, running a trembling paw across his forehead. For all his clever inventions, Archibald Shrew put his own life (and the lives of others) at risk on a regular basis. Something had to be done.

"BIGEYE!" A shout interrupted Mr. Popli's thoughts. The word sent shivers down his tail. Few things struck terror in the citizens' hearts like the monsters below. Unseen, ravenous, unable or unwilling to communicate, the fish made up an entire kingdom of variations on death. The bigeye tuna was a particularly vicious and opportunistic carnivore, and a bobbing shrew would make for an easy meal.

With an acrobatic leap, Mr. Popli sprung back to the top of the wall. He could just make out a dorsal fin slicing the water's surface thirty wavelengths from Archie and closing quickly. The boats would never get there in time.

"Arm the slings!" yelled Mr. Popli. "Bait balls at two o'clock! Distance of sixty waves! Then sixty-five! Lure it away!" He heard the creaking sounds of a ratchet followed by a loud click.

"READY!" a voice cried.

"FIRE!"

A projectile sailed overhead, breaking apart as it descended and showering the water with smaller particles. Bits of rotten food, sawdust, and snail slime made an oily slick of chum on and just below the surface. The bigeye was nearer to the chum than to Archie, but the tuna did not alter course. "It's not turning around!" Merri cheeped.

"Distance of twenty waves!" ordered Mr. Popli. "Fire when ready!" Another bait ball shot past, raining down all around the great fish.

And then the fin disappeared below the surface.

Archie was too busy thinking about death to notice the bigeye. *I wonder which happens first—freezing or drowning? Freezing makes you fall asleep. But if I fall asleep I'll let go of the float and drown. So then would the drowning wake me up from the freezing? I suppose either one is better than being eaten.*

At that moment something slithered past Archie's tail. With a screech, he vaulted out of the water as a ribbed fin exploded the surface right in front of him. The bigeye submerged and then rocketed into the salty air, mouth agape with skewers of teeth each as long as the shrew's whiskers.

Archie looked up, following the fish's arc with awe

as it eclipsed the sun. A giant, gaping mouth flooded his field of vision. *Such amazing teeth!* thought Archie.

As he wondered what kinds of inventions he could create with teeth like those, a yellow blur crashed into him from the side. It was Merri. She'd knocked the wind from them both, but pushed the pair just beyond the bigeye's jaws.

The predator plunged into the sea alongside them and turned for another pass.

Archie and Merri flailed on the water's surface. Only a wave away, they could see the tunafish's eyes burning, hollow and hungry. It raced toward them with frightening speed.

"NOW!" a tiny voice rang out. A small harpoon zoomed through the air and collided with the bigeye in mid-leap, piercing its right eye. The fish flopped once and then descended into the depths.

Strong arms lifted the shrew and the bird into a plastic soda bottle cut in half lengthwise. It was layered with Styrofoam in the bottom, rigged with benches and oars, and painted with a crescent moon down the side. The animals on board the lifeboat all wore crescent moon symbols around their necks, on belts, or on bracelets.

Still too shell-shocked to recognize who had rescued

him, Archie flopped over in the bottom of the vessel. As the waves pounded the side of the boat, his only thoughts were that Merri was alive and they both were safe. The boat ferried them back to the island, and the shivering shrew allowed himself a half smile. *At least I haven't caused any real trouble.*

In fact, Archie's real troubles were just beginning.

Chapter 2

A sheared-off stabilizer from the tail of an airplane bobbed just west of the lagoon, faded vinyl decals cracking and peeling in the midday sun. Crates and boards were stacked on top for shelter from the rain and heat. Sealed-off plastic bottles created pontoons to support the entire structure from below. More boards lay across the ensemble to form access roads for the larger animals. String threaded outward in every direction to create lanes for the smaller, nimbler creatures. The assembly hall had been designed to accommodate every type of animal on the island.

Inside, a consortium of small animals gathered in the public seating area. Mr. Popli stood above the crowd on a platform of various boxes topped with an old, brittle soap dish. Below him, in a cereal bowl decorated with cartoon images of caged circus animals, a miserable-looking Archie Shrew slumped with his head in his paws. He wriggled his snout and looked up, shifting mismatched glasses that allowed him to see slightly better than a cave cricket.

"Order!" announced Captain Shift, a yellow-and-black leopard gecko. "ORDER!" She slapped a strong, thick forelimb against the podium. So many different animals milled below her. She wondered how long this society would last with all of these natural enemies and uneasy truces. And yet somehow Mr. Popli had convinced them to try to live together.

The crowd quieted.

"We are gathered here today to hear testimony about the events of Tuesday, June 7. Mayor Popli will preside."

After a round of polite applause, Mr. Popli addressed the crowd. "Welcome, friends and citizens. It is a happy day indeed." Archie looked up with curiosity. "It is a happy day because we've come so far as a community."

To the left and right of Mr. Popli, a row of venerable-looking animals clicked their pincers, buzzed their wings, and otherwise fidgeted impatiently. "Get on with it, Popli," said a dung beetle whose name happened to be Edward. "We've all got better things to do."

Mr. Popli attempted a smile before continuing. "Since the peace accord, we've built a place where all animals can survive and prosper. I know it hasn't been easy, and I know that our efforts require time that could be spent on equally important responsibilities." He nodded to the dung beetle, who had only come to the meeting because he thought he might get the chance to pronounce punishment on someone.

"This year alone we've designed and constructed three new water towers tall enough to keep out the saltwater spray. A single turnip seed pod, discovered by the eastern geckos, has blossomed into a vast hanging turnip garden. Our algae farm is now protected by netting we've stretched underwater across the entire lagoon. Storehouses are beginning to fill with food as well as reserves of snail slime and fish oil. More of the floating debris has been tied down and converted into homes. We've sworn in twenty new members of the Order of the Silver Moon, and no one has seen even a glimpse of the snake."

A collective shudder shook the room. *Perhaps she's been eaten by a shark*, thought Mr. Popli. The notion filled him with warmth.

"There have, of course, been tragedies. Two drownings. One disappearance. There was the land dispute between the vole clan and the hermit crabs, which had casualties on both sides. And the terrifying four-day battle with that marauding school of tuna. But we citizens are survivors. And, together, we will thrive." More polite applause echoed through the assembly hall.

Mr. Popli hated making speeches, but he knew this was the price of civilization. *And it is a small price to pay compared to how things used to be.*

The mouse continued. "Furthermore, it is a happy day because we are the same number today as we were yesterday. An unfortunate incident put many lives at risk, including a dozen members of the Order of the Silver Moon."

A low grumble spread across the audience and there were several outbursts of "Hear! Hear!" Nearly half of the animals in attendance wore the symbol of a silver moon. Crescents were cut from vinyl, hammered from tin, or gnawed away from bottle caps.

"We invite Archibald Shrew to explain his actions."

"It's about time," mumbled Edward the Dung.

Wringing his tiny paws, Archie adjusted his glasses and stammered, "I . . . um . . . good morning."

"It's afternoon already!" interrupted the dung beetle.

"Ah, yes. Of course," continued Archie, flustered. "Well . . . So . . . So I suppose I erred in the particular dynamics of my latest invention. But the concept is sound, I assure you! Can you imagine the possibilities of a locomotive vessel? We could explore other islands, collect more resources, search for our missing families!" Archie tried not to think of his own family, the smell of burning oil on the air, the sounds of battle.

He looked pleadingly around the room. Archie's list of friends had dwindled—due in part to his obsessive nature but also because of his reputation for getting into trouble. A few sets of eyes met his. Many more glanced down or away.

"And at what risk?" questioned Edward the Dung, looking as smug as if he'd just rolled an exceptionally large ball of poo. "The bird nearly died rescuing you! The fish could've knocked over any of the boats and gobbled up everyone on board! You're lucky it was just one fish. What if it had been a whole school? Or sharks? Or a storm?"

"You could have let me fend for myself," muttered Archie. "I might have made it back safely."

"You seem to miss the point," said Mr. Popli. "When *any* life is in danger, we go out. And your life is no exception."

"I say we banish him!" said Edward the Dung. "Put him on a boat and send him rowing. Good riddance!"

Half the animals applauded. Mr. Popli held up a paw for calm.

"We hold no contempt for you, Mr. Shrew." The mayor sighed. "But you act as though *invention* and *exploration* are more important than your friends and neighbors. And you seem to overlook that we are also inventors, no less skilled than yourself, and our greatest creation is *community*. This community."

Most of the other animals in the room regarded the shrew with mixed expressions of sorrow and pity. But Archie saw only the scowls of indignation and disgust. He wished he could melt, a blur of gray blending into the bright reds and yellows of the cereal dish. Everything Mr. Popli said was true. Archie understood the risks he took. He knew the trouble he'd caused. But he also knew that he couldn't change who he was. *There must be a place in this world for animals like me*, he thought. *But this isn't it.*

Meanwhile, Mr. Popli considered how baffling Archibald Shrew had become. Here was a fellow mammal, also orphaned by the war, forced to claw out a life for himself from the same stinking pile of garbage. Mr. Popli had risen up, working diligently and earning favor with all of the other animals. Archie had not.

From Mr. Popli's perspective, the shrew seemed

to repeatedly slap away every outstretched paw of assistance or friendship. *I don't know how to convince him of the life he could have here*, thought the mayor. *Of what this community could be, if he'd just stick to his work. But all he can think about is inventing—or worse, building ships and going exploring. If one of his crazy contraptions gives everyone hope of something beyond these walls, they'll abandon everything we've worked so hard to build . . . and be fish food in a fortnight. Still, I can't let Edward the Dung have his way. He'd send him rowing off in a teacup with nothing but a thimble of water and wedge of cheese.*

"It is my recommendation that Mr. Shrew's workshop be boarded up and that he be compelled to spend his evenings at the Watchtower," said the mayor. "If he proves dedicated to his expanded duties after three months, we will explore an end of his probation and full restoration to our community."

Archie gasped.

"Unless of course there are others who wish to speak."

The shrew looked dejectedly around the room and, lastly, behind him and up at Merri, who perched in the shadows behind the assembled citizens. The warbler cleared her throat with a high chitter and flitted down. "I would remind the assembly of Archie's past valor and current usefulness.

"Before you judge Archie too harshly, let's not forget the story of how he spied an egg from the top of the Watchtower, floating amidst a school of jellyfish; how he dove heedlessly into certain danger to bring the egg ashore; and how, that very night, I hatched from that egg."

The audience mumbled assent. Merri went on.

"Beyond that, who discovered how to collect and store the rainwater? Archie. Who developed the hydroponic gardens to supplement your nutrition? Archie. And whose idea was it to grease the outer wall with oil and snail slime so the snake could not climb over? It was Archie's idea. Is he at times reckless? Yes. Do his ideas always work? No. But many of the innovations that have added safety and comfort to your lives are due to Archie Shrew." Louder applause. Archie's bushy eyebrows lifted and he looked hopefully up at the council.

"Perhaps," answered Edward the Dung. "But how many of us come back half-starved from his expeditions to gather materials? Too many! And who gets bullied into hard labor to build his ridiculous contraptions? We all do. Everything this shrew does costs more than it's worth. And this latest invention nearly cost a number of lives. He's a bad egg and we should toss him!"

The audience erupted. Some in attendance might

have tried to pitch Archie over the wall for good, right then and there, if not for Mr. Popli.

"Citizens!" squeaked the mouse, banging a clawed fist against the lectern. "We can't banish Archibald. Not yet."

"Why not?" rang Edward's angry voice.

"Because we're not barbarians! We don't throw someone over the wall just because we don't like them. We have rules that protect all of us from that sort of uncivilized behavior." *Does Edward the Dung really want to go back to the way things were? When everyone fought over everything? When only the strongest had enough food to eat and homes to live in? Perhaps he does.*

"Besides, the summer storms will be here any day and we've got a dozen projects we need Archibald to finish. Unless of course there's someone else who will volunteer to do his work? Who wants to take his place scraping algae off the barnacle patches? Or harvesting and bottling the snail slime?"

The only animals who didn't cringe at the thought of bottling snail slime were the snails.

"Again, I propose that we add to Archibald's responsibilities for the next three months. He can continue to do all his regular work. And instead of tinkering in his workshop at night, he can give the rest of you a break by spending his evenings in the tower on storm watch. At the end of three months, if he hasn't changed his ways, perhaps we can allow Mr. Dung to load him in a catapult and launch him over the wall."

The citizens erupted in an accord so loud that even Edward the Dung didn't argue.

"Three months," said Mr. Popli. "NO INVENTING. On storm watch every night. If anyone disagrees with this recommendation, let them speak now."

The only forthcoming sound was the rustling of small animals and, if anyone could hear it, the pitter-patter of Archie Shrew's racing heart.

Chapter 3

A week into his punishment for the sea-cycle incident, Archie had taken to his new routine with all the enthusiasm of a one-armed starfish. During the day, he did everything that was asked of him, but the work made him hungry, and the hunger made him grumpy. And still, his yearning for his workshop rose in his throat each evening like the moon in the sky.

Merri had come to visit Archie each night at the Watchtower. She was the only bird left on Garbage Island. He was the only shrew. In many ways, they were kindred. But Merri was an outsider because of her species. And she was sure that Archie was treated as an outsider because of his actions. If she could get him to see that, perhaps his life could improve. Her attempt to convince him turned into another argument.

"Please, oh wise and annoying bird, tell me the point I'm missing."

"The point, Archie, is that you *could* have a meaningful life here."

"And what if I don't want a meaningful life here? I can't just fly off into the horizon like you, now can I? At least you have the option."

Merri thought about the horizon. How it never got any closer, no matter how fast or far she flew. How every barb of every feather told her she belonged somewhere beyond it. And yet she always turned back toward Garbage Island. Was it fear that kept her from racing into the unknown? Or something else?

"You don't get it, do you?" she asked. "I've been as far and wide as you could sail in a week. The only thing out there is a slow death from exposure or, if you're lucky, a quick one in the jaws of one of the many creatures that would happily eat you."

"And?"

"At least there's a chance at survival here. And for you, there's a chance of belonging. Is it perfect? No! But it's something. And it's better than the nothing out there."

There is something out there, thought Archie. *My family.*

Peace had been declared three days after Archie lost his family. The young shrew had been the last in line

31

behind his other siblings at the end of a head-to-tail caravan led by his mother. He never knew if it had been the reptiles or the birds or even a complete accident that broke apart his family's tiny island. But Archie knew if he held on to his sister's tail any longer, they'd both go tumbling into the freezing winter water. So he let go. He remembered watching everyone he loved drift farther and farther away, tiny eyes peering out from hiding places in the trash, a battle raging between them.

He'd grown up in the aftermath of the war, one of too many orphans amidst too few resources. As a shrew he had to eat every four hours to avoid starvation, and rations weren't enough. He'd been caught stealing, and eventually, folks would turn him away without even a "good morning." He ate things no one else would consider. He spent every night shivering in a different Styrofoam cup or plastic bottle.

The years went on and life improved on the island. Because of his knack for building useful things, the citizens tolerated his voracious appetite and eccentric personality. But Archie never gave up hope that his family was still alive somewhere. *Outside the wall.*

"You could live a good, long life here on Garbage Island." Merri's words seemed to bounce off the shrew like raindrops on rubber. "Just think about it, okay?"

Archie turned his back toward Merri. *It's the only thing I think about.* His stomach growled. *Well, except when I think about food.*

The two sat silently for a long, long time. A gray mist rose up from the ocean and settled between them.

Merri flew away, leaving behind a half-ration of sun-dried barnacles for her friend.

« »

The morning sun peeked over the horizon, and Merri landed at Mr. Popli's houseboat. As the mouse prepared his morning tea, they debated the severity of Archie's punishment.

"He means well, Mayor Popli. He only wants to go searching for his family."

"He's obsessed."

"Can you blame him? What if you had watched as your brothers and sisters floated away? He thinks they're out there somewhere. I have never known my family. Neither have you."

Mr. Popli didn't correct her, but he *could* remember his family in bits and pieces. His father's long whiskers and kind, confident smile; his mother's wise green eyes and the purple shawl she liked to twist with her tail. Those images haunted his dreams, muddied by the yellow of a plastic egg and then always, always shattered by the sound of hissing and a streak of fangs.

33

"For all the danger he put us in, Archibald is lucky he wasn't banished."

"They wouldn't! You know as well as I do that this island would fall apart without Archie."

"You may think that, and I may tend to agree with you. But do the other citizens? I doubt it. I did what I could for him. The matter is closed."

"Yes, Mayor."

Merri left the mouse to his breakfast, fluttering up to, over, and beyond the wall. She climbed skyward—higher and higher until Garbage Island was just a speck below her in a vast field of turquoise blue with sunrise hints of red and orange. *Ten minutes of flapping, and they'd never see me again. No more assignments. No more suspicious looks from citizens. No more saving Archie from his own crazy inventions. I wouldn't even have to say good-bye.*

She'd been miles in every direction. She'd seen other garbage patches, some even with scurrying signs of life. But the warbler never touched down on those other islands. She'd heard too many stories of how clans treated strangers during the war. *How they treated the birds.*

Blown off course and lost at sea, a population of nonmigratory fliers had taken up permanent residence among the garbage. But then a war had broken out between animal clans on the various garbage patches. Birds who flew away to escape the conflict were never heard from again. Those who joined the fight were highly valued mercenaries. Faster and stealthier than the land animals, they terrorized enemy populations. However, the armies learned to fight back. Against arrows and catapults, the avian population dwindled and eventually disappeared.

The memory of those bird attacks lingered, though. To this day, some citizens scowled at the sky when Merri's silhouette flitted overhead, rushing their children away if she landed nearby. She wanted to believe the citizens meant her no ill will, but their actions too often made her feel like a stranger in their land.

As for the migrating sooty shearwater and arctic tern, Merri occasionally heard their cries in the distance. She'd seen a flock on only one occasion and had chased it for half a day. But they were too fast and Merri hadn't stored enough fat to risk a journey of unknown distance by herself. Exhausted, she'd lost sight of them against the horizon and turned dejectedly for home.

My nesting grounds are out there. But even if I could

eat enough to make the journey and fly fast enough to join
a migration, could I really leave Garbage Island? She'd
asked herself that question a hundred times, and every
time the answer was the same.

Yes.

And yet, she banked and turned back to the only
home she'd ever known.

Chapter 4

Maybe I should just leave, thought Archie the next night, flinging pebbles into the sea. Ripples from the stones created undulating circles of bluish black and bright, creamy white. *Or maybe I'll cut the main line and watch as the whole island drifts apart. It would serve them right!* He felt guilty thinking such mean thoughts. He cared about the other animals. But nobody seemed to care about Archie. Except maybe Merri.

True to his word, Mr. Popli had boarded up Archie's workshop and secured it with a padlock he'd scavenged from the stateroom of a half-sunken ship. Even Archie couldn't open it without the key, which Mr. Popli had ordered Merri to keep in her nest, out of the shrew's reach. Dust was settling on Archie's drawings and notebooks as well as on his tools and useful materials.

At the top of the Watchtower, the shrew collapsed onto his back and drew a paw across his eyes, exhausted after toiling through the day. Summer storms would come soon and much preparation had to be done. That afternoon alone he had replaced a rotten panel of the outer wall, oiled the bell, added a new row of rubber tubing in the turnip garden, and checked for weaknesses in a distant section of the main line.

Untethered, garbage patches shifted endlessly at the whim of the ocean currents. But when the animals discovered they could thread cords through and around the flotsam, more permanent structures became possible. Main lines were the strongest of those threaded cords, braided from fishing line, castaway ropes, and plastic bags. A main line encircled an entire island so that no piece or patch could float away. The wall protected the island from outsiders, and the main line held the wall together.

To keep up his pace of work, Archie had eaten more than half his body weight in barnacles and dried algae that day. Still, his stomach gurgled hungrily—everyone was on short rations till the summer storms brought rain and their gardens could produce a harvest.

Archie hungered to invent even more than he hungered for food though. It was only the eighth day of his probation, and he'd already had just as many ideas for useful things that he was not allowed to make.

His snout twitched constantly with irritation. Mostly he'd dreamed up sweeping contraptions that promised to revolutionize society. He dared not sketch those out, except to catalogue the concepts within his prodigious memory. But one idea nagged at him. Like a fish in a net, it flopped about in his mind demanding to be set free.

Better not, Archie, he told himself. *You'll only end up in bigger trouble than ever!*

Archie's paw reached into an outside pouch of his satchel and came across something that should not be there. It was a piece of glass, almost perfectly round and convex. He'd tried not to pick it up when he'd seen it among the rubble on the way to the turnip garden. He'd struggled not to grind it smooth with a porous stone and polish it with bits of cotton. But curiosity had gotten the better of him then, and now more than ever Archie's idea itched like a mosquito bite at the corners of his imagination.

From the main satchel compartment, he retrieved a section of retracting antenna from a television set. At the smallest end of the metal piping, he placed the convex glass. Then, looking around to make sure no one else was afoot, he carefully removed a lens from his glasses and placed it on the larger end of the tube. Both pieces fit snugly with a little wrestling and careful coaxing from Archie's nimble claws. A few judicious taps from a stone and he'd bent the edges of the tube inward to keep the glass from moving.

The idea had come from an image he'd noticed on a plastic case marked "DVD." A hairless monster had stood at the prow of an enormous ship, looking through a similar retractable tube at another ship in the distance. *It must make things appear closer*, thought Archie. And as he considered how light bends as it passes through glass and prisms and even the water, he had an idea for exactly what he would need to build a telescope.

Archie would go on to regret that he'd found the perfect piece of glass on this day of all days. He'd go on to wish he hadn't assembled it at this hour of all hours. If he'd overcome his instinct to invent, even for five minutes, things might well have turned out differently.

But the shrew could not help himself. He whooped with joy when he put the telescope up to his eye and beheld the moon—it brimmed with crags and craters invisible to the naked eye. And the stars! They'd never been so clear! He beheld the Sunset Star and the Jellyfish and Shark Fin constellations—all bright as torches. What's more, in between blazed hundreds of stars and groupings he'd never before seen but recognized from a waterproof navigational chart that filled two entire walls of his workshop. This "looking glass" technology would change everything—navigation, security, storm watching.

And then Archie looked down toward the water and stifled a scream.

There, swimming confidently along the surface, was a massively round and substantially long sea snake. *Colubra!* thought Archie. *I've got to sound the alarm!* Looking again, he noticed a lifeless shape in Colubra's mouth. *Oh, no! The poor soul*, he thought. *I hope it's no one I know. No—wait—what is she carrying?* He adjusted the telescope and saw, to his horror, that Colubra held an egg between her jaws, and she swam it calmly in the direction of her lair.

What to do? What to do?! thought Archie. *If I sound the bell, they'll want to see for themselves. And the only way they'll be able to see is if I show them in the looking glass. But then they'll know I've been inventing, and I'll be in even more trouble!*

The shrew squirmed hesitantly at the top of the Watchtower. A wave rolled against the wall and he fumbled the telescope, nearly dropping it over the side toward the boats moored below. *Or perhaps . . .* thought Archie, *perhaps I can set things right* and *prove Mr. Popli wrong.*

And so Archie Shrew abandoned his post, climbing

down from the Watchtower. *This will never work.* He climbed back up. *Three months! I can't waste three months up here.* He climbed down again. *They'll never forgive me.* Back up once more. Archie continued this conversation in his head, climbing up and down the Watchtower till he found himself out of breath at the bottom. *It has to work.*

The only animal who knew about the secret door in the wall was the clever shrew who'd put it there in the first place. When he'd helped design and supervise the wall's construction, Archie hadn't known when or why he might need a secret door, but it seemed like a useful thing to have. So he'd built it—secretly, of course.

Heart racing, Archie led a narrow skiff down a short passage near the base of the Watchtower that appeared to be a dead end. There, on the back wall, he spun a board on a rusty nail and poked it at just the right spot. A panel swiveled open to the splash of waves.

Pushing the skiff out into the open water, he leapt aboard and closed the door almost all the way with his short, agile tail. As Archie rowed into the inky night, a gust of wind brushed back the fur on his face. Behind him, the secret door creaked open.

Chapter 5

The way Archie had heard the story, the mouse colony never stood a whisker's chance in a windstorm. Because of all the fighting between animal clans, they'd taken up residence in a half-sunken refrigerator made buoyant by its foam insulation. Gnawing through the plastic between the fridge and freezer, they created a secure complex of family apartments. It had been a perfect home—cooled in the hot summers by the temperature of the water and warmed in winters by the sun's rays. It was strong and safe on all sides, and the ice maker was the only way in or out. Except when battles raged nearby, they kept the ice maker's small door propped open to let in fresh air. Other garbage surrounded the old refrigerator, and the mice tethered it all together with a main line.

One day, a weathered aluminum lunchbox drifted into their patch of garbage. The box was trimmed in red and decorated with spaceships spewing red and green firebolts. In the forefront of the firefight, a menacing black helmet loomed. If anyone had taken notice of the lunchbox, they might have barely made out the words ARTH VADER.

The story went on that Colubra had slithered out of the lunchbox and in through the ice maker. Few survivors were ever found. In the mad flight to escape from the colony, a mother and father mouse cradling their baby had to double back through the freezer to evade Colubra. They just missed the last escape boat. As they watched the ship shrink into the distance, they carefully placed an infant Mr. Popli into half of a plastic Easter egg. His mother covered him with a purple shawl and pushed him out into the current. They were never seen again.

To this day none of the animals would venture in the direction of the desolate mouse colony. *None of the animals but me*, thought Archie as he rowed within sight of the refrigerator. Still a hundred waves away, the shrew winced when he clanged an oar against a metal pipe hidden by the water and the dark.

The refrigerator loomed high above the shrew, its former white exterior now overgrown with wet algae that looked black in the moonlight. Gooseneck barnacles clung to the sides below the water line and rust pockmarked all the bits that had once been shiny metal. Archie heaved against the oars one last time and beached the skiff into a mass of plastic bags that had collected around the island. He swallowed hard and wondered, not for the last time, if perhaps he should have stayed in the Watchtower.

Too late to turn back now, he thought, lifting his eyes toward the refrigerator and climbing out of the skiff. At the highest point of the refrigerator, rising into the night sky like a totem, the ARTH VADER lunchbox glared down, wedged between the fridge and an old wooden bed frame.

The shrew had chosen what he thought to be the safest approach to Colubra's garbage patch. A bridge of driftwood and seaweed connected the refrigerator with the jumble of debris where he'd wedged the skiff. *Excellent planning, Archie. At least you'll be safe till you get inside.*

Archie took one step and sank immediately up to his neck in a plastic bag. He yelped and flailed about, but the thin plastic was not dense enough to support the shrew. Thus would have ended his adventure if not for his tail and a chopstick. Archie's thrashing tail found the floating utensil and leveraged it quickly for balance. With effort, he maneuvered the chopstick across the mess of plastic and then pulled himself paw over paw till he reached more stable footing.

Archie shook the water out of his fur and trembled. *Colubra must know I'm here now*, he thought. The shrew looked around for a place to hide but saw none.

Then, to his horror, a creaking sound reached his ears. It came from the ice maker.

Archie's heart raced at an astonishing pace, and as his shrew defenses kicked in, he released a foul-smelling odor meant to keep predators away. Every muscle tensed. Nothing happened. *Must've been the wind*. Slowly, Archie's ears and tail began to relax hair by hair.

And then Colubra's head emerged. Her tongue flicked rapidly as she smelled the air. Archie clenched his jaw to keep from chirping. *I hope that old Popli feels terrible when he finds out I got eaten*, thought the shrew. *It is his fault after all*. The shrew stiffened his back and stood still as the moon—shoulders to his ears and eyes squeezed shut. He waited for the end.

But Colubra paid no attention to the intruder. Turning away from the shrew, she descended the opposite side of the refrigerator. Stymied, Archie wondered what had happened. *Did my smell scare her*

away? Or maybe she's already eaten the egg and she's full? Or still hungry and going back for more? It's not safe out here, that's for certain. So the shrew scrambled up the side of the refrigerator, through the ice maker, and into Colubra's lair.

Archie believed the stories he'd heard of the mouse colony before Colubra, but still he tensed and shivered to see evidence of the desolation. A single beam of moonlight shined through the ice-maker door. In its pale glow, Archie glimpsed mouse-sized artifacts littering shelves and drawers—cups and plates and tools and beds, even toys and dolls bereft of owners to play with them.

The last thread of moonlight touched the edge of Colubra's nest, built with more remnants of the lost mouse civilization. Archie recognized bits of torn clothing mixed with shredded woven mats and even an entire mouse-sized boat that had been splintered and shattered. In the center of the nest he spied the egg. *Ha!* thought the shrew. *She hasn't eaten it yet. She must be waiting for it to hatch.*

As if responding to Archie's idea, a slight rustling sound echoed through Colubra's lair. He scrambled over to the egg, and putting his furry cheek up against the leathery white shell, he felt something moving inside. "Hello there," he said, momentarily forgetting the danger. "Let's get you someplace a little safer."

Archie carefully carried the egg back across the desolate lair, stumbling over the tattered remains of a dress that had once been bright blue. He stifled a scream as a bone crunched under a paw. At long last Archie's twitching nose poked out through the ice maker, scenting for any sign of Colubra. But only the faintest whiff of the snake hung in the dead midnight air.

She's gone! thought the shrew. *Thank goodness. This rescue might be successful after all.*

Archie scrambled backward out of the refrigerator, keeping the egg trapped between his snout and the slippery plastic. He got stuck for several harrowing seconds with his front paws clinging to the lip of the ice maker, not sure how to scale down without dropping the egg. In the end he just let go, both shrew and egg sliding swiftly. The egg plopped onto the same mass of soggy plastic bags that had nearly drowned Archie. And Archie splashed into the ocean—right into Colubra's coils.

The shrew scratched and bit at the snake's skin surrounding him, releasing his own paralyzing venom from small, pointy teeth. He thrashed, clawing and chomping at everything. Fighting furiously, he waited for the sting of Colubra's jaws.

That sensation never came.

Near exhaustion, Archie found a splinter of driftwood with one of his paws. He hauled himself up. He kicked over to the egg, and after wrestling it from the plastic, he swam back to the skiff. There, he heaved the egg and then himself over the side.

Did I kill Colubra? he wondered. *Perhaps I have! I'll be a hero when I haul her body back to the island, and that Mr. Popli will owe me quite an apology. Perhaps I'll forgive him. Once I've shown off the telescope and we've built new and better ships, perhaps I'll let him serve tea on our maiden voyage.*

With renewed energy, Archie rowed the skiff back to the refrigerator and looked for signs of the snake. There, just below the surface, moonlight glinted off a long, scaly body. Archie reached down with an oar and lifted, much to his surprise, a flimsy, all-but-transparent outline of Colubra, like a suit she might have slipped off. *She shed her skin!* thought Archie. *Well, that explains why she never fought back.*

The shrew pulled the snake skin into his skiff and checked the egg one last time. He helped himself to a dozen fresh barnacles from the side of the refrigerator, satiating his hunger for now. Then he set oars for home, completely unaware of the calamity he brought with him.

Chapter 6

When the island broke apart, Archie was not completely to blame.

"Archibald!" Mr. Popli called, banging on the shrew's door. "Archibald Shrew, wake up!"

Archie opened his door and blinked in the early sunlight. "Sorry, Mr. Popli. Those late nights on the Watchtower seem to have caught up with me. I overslept. Did you bring breakfast?"

"Never mind that," said Mr. Popli, nosing his way past the shrew into Archie's front room. "We've got a catastrophe on our hands. Angus woke up this morning to find a school of frogfish in the algae garden—it'll be near impossible to clear them out! How could it happen? You said that if we added your netting contraption to the wall, not even a minnow could squeeze its way through."

"Not even a wedge of turnip?"

"Archibald! How can you think about food at a time like this?!"

"I always think about food," said Archie soberly. "And I can't imagine how the frogfish got in. I inspected every inch of the netting last week. And the outer wall is solid as wood! There's not a whisker of space between any two pieces. Unless . . ." He thought back to the night before, arriving home hours later to find his secret door wide open.

"Unless what?"

"Unless . . . um . . . unless that old cigar box that we used to patch the north wall came loose," Archie lied. "That would've given those frogfish just enough room to wiggle their way into the lagoon."

"Snakespit," said Mr. Popli. "I suppose that could have done it. You're sure there's nothing else it could have been?"

"No. Not—um. Nothing, Mayor Popli."

Such a terrible liar, thought the mouse. *What are you hiding, Archibald Shrew?* "Carry on, then. I'll go and check the wall myself." The mouse turned to leave. "And Archibald?"

"Yes?"

"You've somehow managed to lose another lens in your glasses."

"I know. Unfortunate incident at the Watchtower."

"Well, go ahead and fix them if you can. I won't keep you from that. Besides, how much damage could you do tinkering with a tiny piece of glass?"

"Not much, I'm sure."

《 》

Mr. Popli felt most at home on a boat by himself, untethered to the mainland. Now a sense of liberation overcame him each time his skiff climbed to the crest of a wave and then sped down into the trough of the next. For a moment, he wished the island didn't exist at all and he could just look out for himself.

You can't afford to be so selfish, he scolded. *If you don't keep everyone working together, the whole island could fall apart.*

He gripped the oars with small, strong paws and pulled against the current. *This must be the way Archibald always feels. Fewer real responsibilities than a fruit fly and all the time in the world for his little inventions.* He suddenly wondered if he was jealous of the shrew. No, he most certainly wasn't. If not for Merri, Archibald Shrew had hardly a friend in the ocean. And all the foulest jobs that no one else would do. *Whenever Archibald bottles snail slime you can smell him coming for days afterward.*

The supposed loose panel in the outer wall was only

accessible by rowing around the island, and the task would take all morning. By the time he reached the panel, he'd already devoured his lunch. He'd planned to make a fine snack of any loose barnacles along the way, but it looked as though Archie had picked them all when he'd completed the work previously. Grumbling to no one in particular, Mr. Popli tied his skiff to the wall.

I wonder how badly that shrew has botched this job, he thought. *Probably hammered in two nails and then spent the rest of the day loafing.*

The half-submerged panel, a cigar box lid, was weathered nearly beyond recognition. Patches of color on it revealed the remnants of an illustrated landscape— an island girl in a long skirt beckoned toward a sun-kissed field blossoming with banana trees and tobacco plants. To Mr. Popli, who had never seen a tree, much less a person, the picture made no more sense than the spaceships from Colubra's lunchbox that haunted his dreams.

Waves lapped lazily against the wall as Mr. Popli dove into the water. He carried a bag of nails in a belt, a hammer in one paw, and a chisel between his teeth. Strapped to his leg was a long, thin knife fashioned from a shard of broken glass. Sharp as a gill on both edges with a handle made of rubber strapping, it had spilled more blood than Mr. Popli would have preferred. He hoped he wouldn't need it today.

Mentally, the mouse went through an inspection checklist as he climbed portions of the wall and dove down to look at others. He scrutinized every inch of the cigar box and each of the adjoining pieces of the wall. *Lashings—tight but not too tight; knots—secure; wood—no rot or soft spots; main line—some tattering but holding strong in all directions; nails—straight through. But look here; it's a wonder this patch is holding at all! Archibald's put too few nails in it. Still, the frogfish couldn't have come through here. I wonder what Archibald knows that he's not telling.*

Mr. Popli hammered seven more nails into the cigar box and turned for home.

As the mouse made his way back around the point of the island, an unseasonably large wave rolled beneath his skiff, lifting him nearly high enough to see over the wall. *Curious*, he thought, as the wave continued along the wall and out of sight. By then, he was too far away to hear the sharp crack of the cigar box splintering where his fifth nail had been hammered. The two pieces held together for a moment before shearing in half.

Below the split patch, part of the wall dropped down, coming to rest right on an exposed section of the main line. If any of the islanders felt the slight shudder that reverberated through the garbage patch, they dismissed it as the wake from a migrating humpback whale.

Chapter 7

Archie rubbed his backside, sore from sitting on the egg for nearly an hour. It seemed in no hurry to hatch, still wrapped in the shed snake skin and hidden in the short passage near the Watchtower. *It needs to be warmer*, he thought. *And I need a snack! I suppose we'll have to head home.* And so, hoping no one would see him, Archie slipped the skiff and the egg out of the passage and into a canal that led to the lagoon. Halfway home, he nearly collided with the one animal he least wanted to see.

"Hullo there, Archibald!" said Mr. Popli. "Just the shrew I was looking for. The patch is holding fine. Our frogfish problem must've come from somewhere else."

"That's curious news," Archie replied. "But I'm glad to know the patch is holding strong." He pulled even harder on his oars, trying to put distance between himself and the mouse.

But Mr. Popli seemed determined to make conversation and matched his pace.

"We'll need a top-to-bottom inspection of the wall before the summer storms begin, which could be any day. I'll assign Merri and Reginald to collaborate with you on this. They're both hard workers, and Merri's craftsmanship surpasses anyone's. I say—what have you got in your skiff?"

"Nothing!" Archie's voice cracked and he redoubled his rowing. "Nothing at all."

"It doesn't look like nothing," said Mr. Popli, angling his course to intercept the shrew. The egg rested at Archie's feet but poked up high enough to be barely visible. Mr. Popli pulled ahead, parking his skiff directly in Archie's path. The shrew dug his oars into the water, but it was too late. The two boats collided, jarring both animals from their seats. Mr. Popli jumped up, angrier than ever.

"Archibald, what exactly have you been working on today?"

"I, um, well—" Archie began.

"Come with me," Mr. Popli commanded. "And that's an order you'd better obey."

A large wave rolled between them.

《 》

Mr. Popli's houseboat had begun its life as a milk jug at a dairy processing plant in California. After it tumbled from a trash barge in the Port of Los Angeles, it rode the ocean waves for seven months before drifting, barnacled but watertight, into the garbage patch. Mr. Popli had found it on his birthday, and spent months scrubbing it clean and rigging it out.

The squarish milk jug balanced in the water like an ark. The molded plastic handle faced the sky, and, at the end of its nozzle, the porthole pointed toward the lagoon. Outside, Mr. Popli had lashed smaller bottles, some to act as pontoons and some as rain barrels. A butter dish fastened to the rear served as his bathtub. Up top he'd created a sun deck of driftwood. Stretched across the whole ensemble, bits of plastic had been sewn together to form a tarp. The tarpaulin helped protect the houseboat from the sun, and when it rained, it funneled fresh water into the barrels.

Inside, he'd run plastic coffee stirrers across the lower third to form a bottom deck. Precise holes gnawed in the ceiling supported a system of ropes, notched planks, and pulleys that allowed the mouse to perch at nearly any height. With careful knots and thoughtful design, he'd fashioned a hanging bedroom, a living area, and even a tiny box garden where a sugar snap pea plant promised an early harvest. His few pieces of furniture could be moved to and fro by pulling on this rope or that, and everything could be securely battened down for the summer storms.

He'd named his houseboat the *Abigail*, after his mother. He often imagined showing her the vessel, certain she'd be impressed by his hard work and innovation. Today, however, he had no such reveries.

"Eggs and snake skins!" Mr. Popli's voice echoed so loudly it rattled the walls of the *Abigail*. He looked contemptuously at the egg that Archie had brought inside and insisted be wrapped in blankets. He refused to allow the snake skin in, however, leaving it in the loosely tethered skiff outside. Medium-sized waves now rolled through every other minute, but neither took any notice.

"Your ears are turning bright red, Mr. Popli. You might want to calm down."

"I AM PERFECTLY CALM!" The mouse breathed in deeply and gathered himself for a moment. "Perhaps *you* should calm down."

"I'm fine, thank you."

"You should be fine, Archibald Shrew! With your careless, carefree life and fewer actual responsibilities than an inchworm."

"That's unfair! I work harder than anyone else on the island!"

"Doing what? Dreaming all day instead of completing your work?"

"Even if I did, it'd be more than you do, MR. MAYOR! It must be nice to spend your days assigning ridiculous jobs to other animals while you sit around sipping dandelion tea and nibbling poppy seeds.

"'Look at me,'" the shrew mocked in a high-pitched voice, sipping from an invisible cup. "'I'm the *mayor*! Do what I say, or I'll catapult you over the wall!'"

"THAT'S NOT AT ALL HOW I SOUND!"

Archie continued with his impression. "'And besides being insufferable, I'm a ridiculous excuse for a mammal. My tail is too long and I'm missing a toe on each foot.'"

"What? What do you mean my tail is too—oh. I see. Well. Your tail is too short! And quit trying to change the subject, Archibald Shrew! You *will* tell me where this egg came from and how you got it here. And I'll take nothing but the truth!"

And so Archie told the complete story of how he'd gotten the egg. Except for the part about inventing the telescope. And the small detail about the secret door. And the embarrassing bit where he valiantly conquered the snake skin. But other than that, he told the whole truth.

Color rose again in Mr. Popli's ears as Archie spoke. By the time he had finished, Mr. Popli was as red as a bottle cap. "Insubordination! Dereliction of duty!" he shouted. "Did you even think about what would happen if Colubra had seen you? A dozen walls would not keep her out. This time they'll send you away forever, and I won't be able to stop them!"

He paused his tirade to steady himself as the largest wave yet shoved the houseboat up against its mooring. The lashings held firm, and the duo leaned in to the shifting floor until it stabilized.

Just below the split patch on the northern part of the wall, a rusty panel of corrugated steel shifted down even farther, putting all its weight on the main line that held the island together. The undulating waves moved it back and forth like a saw blade.

Archie hadn't considered the repercussions of entering Colubra's lair. But he had saved a life! Mr. Popli had to see that. He wondered what banishment might be like. Perhaps he'd build a new sea-cycle and find his lost family. And what of the egg? Would he be here long enough to see it hatch? Not if Mr. Popli had anything to say about it. Of that he was certain.

A low toll resonated through the houseboat. The duo exchanged glances.

"Is that the bell?" asked Archie.

"It can't be. It sounds too far away."

They dashed to the porthole and gasped in unison. Mr. Popli's houseboat and its mooring floated freely away from the island. The main line had been severed. The island was drifting apart.

Chapter 8

"Snakespit," Mr. Popli cursed. Archie, for once, agreed.

The duo scrambled out of the hatch and climbed the lashings holding the top deck in place. From there they could better see the island; but it was drifting farther away by the minute. And since Mr. Popli had not designed the *Abigail* as a seafaring vessel, she possessed no sails, no oars, no method of locomotion. They were trapped on a floating prison.

Archie suggested that they could swim back, taking turns to push the egg along on a float. Mr. Popli flatly refused, citing every danger from currents to carnivorous fish to Colubra herself, who had probably already entered the city to gobble up each and every citizen in the chaos.

"Well, I hope you've got a better idea," said Archie.

"I may indeed."

Mr. Popli salvaged long, flat sticks from the remains of the mooring platform. Balancing on the water barrels, they paddled furiously back toward the island. After a full ten minutes, Archie gave up.

"We're going nowhere," the shrew shouted across the nose of the houseboat.

"I'm afraid you're right. We need to cut ourselves loose from the mooring platform."

"No—we just need more leverage. Instead of paddling the *Abigail*, let's cut the houseboat loose and paddle the platform."

"We can paddle the platform, but we're not leaving my houseboat!"

They clambered down the tethering rope and onto the mooring platform itself. Made mostly of wood with bits of foam tucked in the cracks, the raft-like platform floated just above the waterline. From here they made better progress, but waves washed over the top, bowling them over and sometimes into the ocean. After a series of long, dark shadows passed beneath them, they retreated from the platform back to the *Abigail*.

"Maybe I could reimagine the tarpaulin as a sail," said Mr. Popli, climbing paw over paw to the top deck. "We could ride the wind back to the island."

"It's blowing the wrong way!" Archie called over his shoulder, scampering along the pontoons.

"I'm going to see if I can finagle it. And Archibald—you'd better not try anything foolish!"

Archie looked toward the shrinking island. He could barely see it now. He decided to try something foolish.

At the back of the houseboat, Archie used his sharp, spiky teeth to slash through the lashings holding Mr. Popli's bathtub in place. He maneuvered the butter dish atop the mooring platform at the front of the boat. By the time Mr. Popli realized Archie was right about the wind, the shrew had loaded the egg and was preparing to row away. Mr. Popli had to tackle him to keep him from succeeding. The duo tumbled into the water and climbed, sputtering, back onto the platform. Archie barely snagged hold of the butter dish before it floated off.

"We're caught in a current, Archibald. No amount of paddling will get us back to the island until we drift out of it."

"But with a small enough vessel I can paddle *across* the current instead of *against* it and probably make it home in time for a snack before dinner."

"Didn't you just eat lunch?"

"I know. But I'm hungry again."

"You're *not* going!"

"I am, and you'd come with me if you cared more about your life than you do this silly houseboat."

How dare he! thought the mouse. Of course he

cared about getting them home safely. But at the same time, his houseboat was far from silly! He'd spent months designing it, redrawing the plans at least a dozen times. Yes, he regularly scrubbed every inch of plastic till it shined. And maybe, just maybe, he had tethered the *Abigail* so far from other homes so he'd have fewer visitors to sully his perfect vessel. But he would gladly let it go if it meant rescuing himself and Archibald. Wouldn't he?

Archie wasn't waiting to find out. "I'll send help when I get back," said the shrew. He'd broken free from Mr. Popli's grip and was pushing away from the platform, using one of his makeshift oars to shove himself into the current.

"You'll do no such thing," said Mr. Popli, snatching ahold of the paddle at the last second. "I'll need your help aboard the *Abigail* once we've drifted out of the current and can paddle back. I can't do it by myself." He hauled the oar toward him until he could grip the edge of the butter dish. With a giant heave, he pulled Archie, egg, and dish back onto the rocking platform.

Archie leapt from the dish and bared his teeth, shoving a clawed finger at Mr. Popli's snout.

"I thought I was banished. So then I don't suppose you're in charge of me any longer. I'll take my chances with my own ideas, thank you very much."

"First of all, you're not banished yet. Second, it's my bathtub and you can't have it! But if you continue to disobey orders, I'll have you chopped into a bait ball, then banished."

"Sounds preferable to spending another minute with you!"

And that's how Merri found them: slip-sliding atop the mooring platform and snarling over a butter dish.

"Archie! Mayor Popli!" Merri lighted on the milk jug's spout.

"Merri," said Mr. Popli finally, composing himself and looking away from Archie. "Thank goodness you've found us. What's happened?"

"The main line—it snapped. Most of the island is so interconnected that it's all stayed in one place, but you've lost a few houses, many of the boats, and part of the wall is sinking. The citizens have pulled back toward the center of the island, and every able-bodied animal is working to repair the damage. You two were the only ones unaccounted for, until now. No one's hurt, but your help is needed. I'll arrange a rescue party to come get you with the big rowboat."

"We're caught in a current, Merri. The rowboat would be in as much trouble as we're in," said Mr. Popli.

"Nonsense," said Archie. "Ten rowers could make

progress against this current. Send them as quickly as possible!"

"You'll do nothing of the sort," said Mr. Popli. "And that's an order. Mark our coordinates, then return to the island. Let the council know what happened, but for goodness' sake make sure Edward the Dung is the last to know. As long as he doesn't get in the way I can coordinate things from here. Bring news and come back to see if we're free of the current."

"Yes, sir."

"Archibald is somehow responsible for this mess."

Merri's beak dropped. Could Archie have really made the island fall apart? He could be warm and kind and fiercely loyal. But she also knew what happened when he couldn't control himself. She'd seen him act selfishly and recklessly and dangerously. He might not have done it on purpose, but he certainly could have severed the main line.

And that's when she saw the egg.

Chapter 9

"What's that?" Merri asked.

Archie and Mr. Popli exchanged glances.

"I . . . I saved it," said Archie. "I was going to tell you."

"Where? How?"

Mr. Popli cut in, hefting the egg out of his bathtub. "Merri, we'll answer all of your questions. But for now you can think of this egg as one more reason to get us home as quickly as possible. Archibald did find it, and somehow in doing so he's caused this disaster. But right now we need your swift assistance before we're all in real danger."

As Mr. Popli wrestled the egg back inside the houseboat, Merri and Archie stood in silence. Archie could not meet her gaze. He turned away to count the hairs on the end of his tail, letting go of the butter dish. Why hadn't he brought her the egg? Maybe he was still upset about their argument. *Or maybe you knew that she'd be the natural choice to hatch an egg. And you wanted to keep it for yourself.*

Mr. Popli climbed back out of the hatch. Merri exchanged a few more words with the mouse, and then flitted off toward the island.

"Well, now you've done it, Archibald," Mr. Popli chided. "You've ruined things even more than I imagined possible!"

"I have, haven't I? I suppose I should have told her."

"Told her? Oh, yes. About the egg. Of course."

"Wait. If you didn't mean the egg, then what were you talking about?"

"Nothing."

"Mr. Popli. We are adrift at sea with no way home, having just deeply offended our only hope of rescue! All of which you think is *my* fault! What else could I possibly have done?"

"There is the small matter of my bathtub."

Squinting against the sun, the duo watched Mr. Popli's butter dish bob farther and farther away until it disappeared into the horizon.

《 》

As she flew, Merri noticed her tiny shadow flickering over the ocean and tried not to think of the egg or of Archie's betrayal. She imagined instead what it must

76

be like to fly in a flock, dozens or even hundreds of shadows soaring in formation. Did other birds play games to pass the time as they flew? What was it like to sleep nestled up with brothers and sisters? Would others think her strange, having grown up with only non-fliers? What if they thought that she flapped her wings funny? Or that her warble sounded a bit like a shrew's squeak?

The stories she'd heard from the citizens all ended the same way. War had discouraged avian life around the islands. Any passing bird might be mistaken for an enemy fighter and attacked. Eventually, they had all died in the fighting or fled in search of safer lands.

But if I was born after *the war, where did I come from? And what about this new egg? There must be a bird colony nearby. Perhaps my family is there, searching for me even now. They could be just over the horizon!*

And then she saw them: dark spots on the water's surface, shadows tracking along at exactly her speed. Merri spun toward the sky, searching. But she saw nothing. *No! Where did they go?* Flying as high as she dared, she darted between clouds, scanning the air with her sharp vision.

She looked back down; the shadows still raced. She dove. The shadows grew. A bull mahi leapt from the water, launching a spray of crystalline droplets into the air. Merri swerved and climbed higher. The green-and-blue fish flopped back into the rushing shadows. *Just a school of fish*. The swarm of mahi wove playfully in and around one another below the waves. *Like a happy family*, thought Merri as she flew on alone.

<< >>

Days passed and the current died down, but tensions did not. By now the rowboats could no longer reach them. The only sailboat large enough to risk the venture had sunk when the island started to break apart. Still, Archie and Mr. Popli made slow progress toward the island. The egg, bundled in blankets in the warmest part of the ship, had not hatched.

As the island grew even the tiniest bit closer, Archie longed to see it up close through the lens of his looking glass. But he left the invention right where he'd hidden it in the big pouch of his satchel. *No doubt Mr. Popli would commandeer it for himself. Besides, it's rather nice to know something he doesn't.*

For her part, Merri made several flights a day back and forth between the island and the *Abigail*. She brought something small but helpful each time she came. An extra length of string. A matchstick. A rubber band. She tried to keep her spirits high, but life on the island had become tense. Without Mr. Popli there to calm tempers, factions had formed. The council argued over how to accomplish the most routine tasks and about which unlucky souls would carry out Archie's rather unpalatable assignments. And while no one was openly hostile toward Merri, she felt a further shift in how the islanders addressed her.

Merri, fix that! Merri, go there! Merri, take this message to Edward. The citizens seemed to need her more than ever, but treated her as a mere errand bird. And though she grew exhausted from her efforts, Merri refused to ask for extra rations or rest. *I'll sleep when Mr. Popli and Archie are home safe.*

She brought news of the progress on the island to the *Abigail*. "The main line snapped on the north end of the island. That's also right where the wall split, but no one can seem to figure out why. They're still working to float that section of the wall high enough up that a new patch can be added. You were there that morning, weren't you, Mayor Popli?"

Mr. Popli's ears lowered, almost imperceptibly. *Snakespit*, he thought. He had hammered the extra nails into the patch. They *could* have split the cigar box lid, and that *might* have had an effect on the main line. "I was there, inspecting Archibald's recent patch, but nothing seemed out of the ordinary," he said eventually. Then he quickly asked about the condition of old Mrs. Toad, whose declining vision caused her to keep eating

79

plastic berries. Archie looked curiously at the mouse but said nothing.

The next morning, Merri landed on the hull of the *Abigail* in an excited flutter. "Mayor Popli! Archie! Come quickly!" She tapped incessantly on the thin plastic. The hatch on the porthole opened, and a pair of harried mammals emerged, climbing to the top deck to meet the bird.

"What is it, Merri?" asked Mr. Popli.

"Whales? Sharks? Whale sharks?!" asked Archie.

"No! But you won't believe what's drifted toward you overnight. You can see it just over there!" They squinted and looked to where Merri was pointing.

"There's something out there for sure," said Mr. Popli. "What is it? More trash?"

Archie recognized it at once. He gasped and then began chittering excitedly. Not more than a hundred lengths away was the wreckage of Archie's sea-cycle. Early morning sunlight glinted off the clear plastic and misaligned coil spring.

"It's my invention!" cried Archie. "The locomotive engine! Merri! Mr. Popli! We're saved!"

Mr. Popli stared hopelessly at the broken-down rig of castaway parts and floating garbage. "Doomed is more like it."

Chapter 10

An hour before the storm struck, the familiar sound of Archie and Mr. Popli arguing woke Merri from her nap. She'd sapped all her strength carrying a pipe nearly as heavy as she was from the island. Archie needed it to finish the steering mechanism, and she had gone after it against Mr. Popli's better judgment. But Archie said they couldn't manage without it and Merri had insisted she could do it. She'd arrived too tired even to speak. They'd had to help her inside.

The wreck had destroyed both the body and front wheel of the sea-cycle. They could not salvage the vessel. But the coil-powered engine along with the remaining paddle wheel had survived and seemed to function.

Archie's solution was to rig the engine at the back of the *Abigail* and steer her home. Mr. Popli flatly refused, of course, but gave in when Archie flatly refused to help paddle unless they spent equal time on his idea.

The mouse's eyes bulged with every smear of grease on the polished hull. He squeaked involuntarily with every new hole that the shrew punctured in the perfect plastic.

Mr. Popli still insisted they spend the first several hours of each day paddling toward the island—just in case the second voyage of Archie's coil-powered engine was as much a failure as the first. They were running low on supplies, and lower still on patience.

To Archie, every minute they spent paddling toward the island was a wasted chance to install the engine. To Mr. Popli, every hour of inventing lessened their chances of ever making it home. And still, the egg had not hatched.

Eventually, Archie lost his patience. "You're a tyrant, which would be fine if you weren't also ridiculous! It will take two extra days to install the steering *inside* the houseboat *and* we won't be able to see where we're going. It's a laughable idea."

"We can cut a hole in the front of the *Abigail* so we can see to steer and I'll replace it with glass later. Installing the steering on top of the houseboat would expose the driver to weather, Colubra's attacks, and who knows what else. And I don't appreciate name-calling, by the way."

"I've got much worse names in mind for you!"

"By all means, do tell," said Mr. Popli, who felt a sudden tinge of satisfaction at seeing Archie lose his temper.

"You're a self-important, stuck-up pig of a mouse!"

"Go on."

"Why you're nothing but a . . . a snake! A skulking, slithering monster who only cares about himself and his precious houseboat!"

"You're just upset because, deep down, you know I'm right and you don't want to admit it."

"Deep down is where you'd be the most useful. I think you'd make an extraordinary anchor." The shrew gestured toward the ocean.

"At least the conversation would be more intelligent. And the company would be far more agreeable."

And that's how Merri found them when she woke: once again bickering—and completely unaware of the storm racing in from the southeast. Billowing clouds were clambering over one another like an angry swarm of black flies. On the opposite horizon, the distant island sparkled under blue skies.

"Mayor Popli," said Merri, poking her head out of the open porthole.

"Not now."

"With all respect."

"I said NOT NOW."

"Perhaps after you sink in the giant storm that's headed straight for us?"

Only then did Archie and Mr. Popli look up. Merri flew from the hatch and lighted on the tarpaulin.

"You know what, Archibald? I think you may be right," said Mr. Popli. "Let's install the steering on top. How quickly can it be done?"

"Thank you for agreeing, Mr. Popli," said Archie, eyes widening at the gathering darkness. "But it could take half a day to cut the steering column to size."

"We're out of time. Is there another way?"

"I could have it done in ten twitches with the pipe saw from my workshop."

"I'll get it," said Merri. "I can go and be back before the storm gets here."

"No!" said Mr. Popli. "You're in no condition to fly. We'll have to manage on our own."

"Let me go," Merri advised. "I feel fine. Besides, we haven't heard the bell! With all the chaos of the past few days, there's been no one on storm watch. Someone needs to warn the citizens!"

Archie knew it was dangerous. He knew she was tired. He wanted to agree with Mr. Popli and tell her to stay. But as much as he cared for his friend, he wanted to finish his invention. He wanted to race the storm and win. He wanted the thrill of taking nature by the gills and beating her with his own cleverness. He looked pleadingly at Merri. She'd never been able to say no to that look.

Merri leapt into the sky and performed a somersault. With the sun shining and the wind at her back, the black clouds seemed a distant threat. She landed on the edge of the porthole.

Mr. Popli considered Merri for a moment and appeared satisfied that she was fit to fly. "Go then," he said. "Sound the bell. Get Archibald's tool. But promise me you'll stay put if the storm moves in too quickly."

"Aye, aye, Mayor." Merri and Archie exchanged a final glance. "Besides, what's the worst that could happen?"

Mr. Popli called after her as she sped away, "If you hear thunder, don't come back for us. It will be too late."

Twenty minutes later, Archie and Mr. Popli strained their eyes and ears toward the island, urging the bell to signal Merri's safe arrival. Ten minutes after that they began to worry. It shouldn't have taken this long. Archie thought again of the telescope belowdecks. Should he get it even though he'd have to explain everything to Mr. Popli? He longed for a sound from the bell, one toll that meant Merri had made it back safely. Thunder crackled overhead. Lightning illuminated the waves. The bell never rang.

The wind gusted in earnest now. Stinging raindrops lashed against the *Abigail*, driving the duo belowdecks. Lightning crashed overhead, and rain fell in thick sheets. The ravenous storm, it seemed, would swallow the houseboat whole.

Mr. Popli had designed the *Abigail* with extreme conditions in mind. Between the ballast inside and the water barrels fastened outside, she was nearly impossible to flip. Even if the hull was punctured, her pontoons would keep her afloat. But a big enough wave could send her rolling or even crush the hull like a soda can. And if they lost buoyancy in both the pontoons and the hull, she'd fill up with water and join the lost wreckage at the bottom of the sea.

Instinct and experience propelled both the mouse and the shrew—the pair tightened ropes, adjusted ballast, and stowed anything that hadn't been tied down. Still, they never would have purposefully set out in an untethered, unsteerable vessel in a squall. Many of Mr. Popli's possessions were sent flying and dashed to pieces, and his tail got an awful pinch between two planks that weren't properly tied down. Archie dropped his glasses and earned a nasty gash across his leg while scrambling down to collect them.

Waves tossed the *Abigail* for hours. Mr. Popli held

on tightly to whatever he could find, using a free paw or tail to defend himself from lashing ropes and crashing boards. The egg was in constant jeopardy, even though it was wrapped in blankets and held down with rubber bands. Archie protected it at his own peril, often using his body to ward off the flying debris.

As the storm buffeted the houseboat, both its passengers tried not to think about Merri. Neither was successful.

The thunder boomed in the distance. The torrent became a drizzle, and, finally, the sun came out. The *Abigail* had held together through the storm. The same could not be said of Archie.

"Merri," he whimpered through chattering teeth as Mr. Popli bandaged his leg. Head buried in his paws, the shrew rocked back and forth.

"She could have made it," said Mr. Popli. "What we have to do now is get home. I'm sure we'll find her there." The words tasted like lies, even as he said them.

But Archie made no response.

And to make matters worse, the horizon stretched out in a line as flat and straight as a coffin lid. The island had disappeared from sight.

Chapter 11

Snakespit! Mr. Popli swore to himself as a thin metal strap slipped from between his teeth, bouncing off the side of the houseboat and into the water. It was the second one he'd dropped. If he lost even one more, there wouldn't be enough to finish installing the steering. *Too many mistakes*, he thought, angry with himself. *Perhaps I should take a break.* Without Archie's help, he was failing miserably at making the *Abigail* locomotive.

Hunger made him ill-tempered, but he wouldn't allow himself to eat. They'd been adrift for five days now, and Mr. Popli's houseboat had been well-stocked with enough to feed one mouse for several weeks. *But that shrew eats three times as much as I do!* he thought. Of fresh water, they had plenty. The storm had filled all of the water barrels to the top. One had been punctured and contaminated with salt water, leaving seven barrels of good water. But with no further deliveries from Merri . . .

Merri, he thought.

When the birds had vanished at the end of the war, Mr. Popli wondered if they'd ever return. And then came Merri. Of course he didn't believe Archibald's ridiculous story of how he'd valiantly rescued her, diving into the flotsam from the top of the Watchtower. But still . . .

Mr. Popli had been there on the day she hatched, featherless, unprotected. Having never raised a family, he felt nearly as helpless. He'd worried as much as Archibald had on the day she learned to fly. How his stomach lurched when she leapt from her perch and soared over their heads! He'd presided on the day she joined the Order of the Silver Moon, tearing up as she— the most courageous, intelligent, and willing to serve of all the recruits—warbled her oath. Grudgingly, the other islanders accepted her as a citizen. He knew that some citizens still looked on her with fear, but wasn't that the whole point of their community? That predator and prey could live together? Merri was a symbol of that hope.

And now she might be gone, thought the mouse. *Perhaps it would be better if I stayed gone as well. What have I really accomplished? Peace? Safety? Community?*

It's all hanging together by a whisker. I'm just as much of a dreamer as Archibald with his wild inventions. At least his contraptions seem to work once in a while.

He got a drink of water, then went to check on Archie.

After the storm, the shrew had climbed into a bunk and had barely moved since. He suffered from much more than hunger and physical exhaustion. If grief and guilt had overcome Mr. Popli in a wave, they'd sucked Archie down like a whirlpool.

In his peculiar way, Archie saw Merri as his adopted child, as family. He'd fed her from his own paws, raised her in his workshop as his own. He'd never understood her desire to join the Order of the Silver Moon. But, like a father, he wanted her to follow her dream, not his. He marveled at how she grew—curious, artistic, independent. She seemed invincible; Archie never thought he'd live to see her gone.

"Archibald," said Mr. Popli, shaking the shrew not unkindly. "I've done all I can with the steering. I must have your help to finish. The longer we drift the less likely we'll be able to find the island again."

Archie didn't reply.

"Come on, now! What would Merri think of you moping around like this? What if she did make it back, and she's been zipping all over the ocean looking for us? It would be quite rude of us not to go and meet her halfway."

Archie looked up at the sound of Merri's name. "You think she might be?"

"Honestly, I don't know, Archibald. She's a stout bird, strong as a mackerel and stubborn as—well—stubborn as you. If a great white shark tried to snatch her from the air, she'd peck his eyes out and eat them for dinner. Don't you think?"

"That sounds like Merri all right." Archie smiled just a little.

"Well, should we head home then? See if she's waiting for us with a cup of tea?"

"Okay."

Standing up from the bunk, Archie limped through the ship and out of the porthole hatch.

By the time the sun set, the *Abigail* was ready to be driven and steered from an open-air cabin under the tarpaulin on the top deck. Working together they'd cut and installed the steering column, even devising a rather clever automatic brake system that promised to keep the paddle wheel turning at a prescribed rate. Bit by bit, the work had reignited the shrew's spirit.

Archie sulked only a little when he realized his wounded leg would make him unable to pedal and pilot the houseboat. And so the duo held their breath as Mr. Popli turned the pedals with his legs, winding the coil spring. "Here goes nothing," he said, pulling a lever to release the brake.

When indeed nothing happened, two sets of whiskers and tails drooped side by side.

"I double-checked everything," said Archie. "It ought to be working."

"Maybe you should have triple-checked."

"Maybe *you* should—" Archie stopped and turned his head sideways. "Maybe you should pull on the brake release instead of the steering lever."

"Oh! Right."

Mr. Popli did. And there was a click. And another. And the paddle wheel at the back of the *Abigail* began to turn. As it pushed water away, the houseboat began to move forward. Mr. Popli carefully pulled the steering lever to the left. The *Abigail* veered right. He pulled right. The houseboat went left. "Ha ha!" he cried. "We've done it, Archibald! We've done it! We'll be sipping tea on the island tomorrow."

Mr. Popli had never been more wrong.

« »

Using the stars to navigate, they headed north through the twilight. The ocean at night came alive in hundreds of different ways. In and through the waves they heard the splashes of fish and even the distant songs

95

of whales. The water reflected not only the moon and stars, but glowing algae and schools of jellyfish. The sea looked like a painting and the *Abigail* was the tiniest brushstroke streaking across it.

But the biggest change was between Mr. Popli and Archie. They spoke more to each other as they sailed than they'd ever talked before. Archie chittered continuously, telling stories of the inventions that had blown up in his face and the ones he'd thought of but never built. Mr. Popli, for his part, talked about the rigors of managing a community and how difficult some of the citizens could be at times. He even told a joke, at which Archie laughed hysterically.

By morning the island was still nowhere on the horizon. "The storm must have blown us farther off course than I imagined," said Mr. Popli. "Is there any way to figure how far we've come?"

"I suppose," said Archie, "but it would only make a difference if we knew exactly where we were going and had been calculating our position at regular intervals."

"We've got to be close!" said Mr. Popli. "How likely is it that we passed by the island in the night without ever seeing it?"

"It's possible. Likely, too."

"If only we had some way of seeing farther into the distance."

"What if I told you we did?"

He leapt down from the top deck and scrambled into the quarters below. He returned triumphantly with the telescope he'd invented and explained it to Mr. Popli.

"So this is what happened to your glasses," the mouse guessed.

Archie grinned sheepishly.

Still, Mr. Popli marveled as he looked through the telescope. "I think you're on to something, Archibald. We definitely came too far east."

"What makes you say that? The sargassum patch we passed on the second day? The fabled rubber ducky flotilla?"

"No." Mr. Popli pointed into the distance and handed Archie back the telescope. "The island."

Chapter 12

The next time they nearly died, it was definitely Archie's fault. Exhausted from pedaling the *Abigail* toward the island, Mr. Popli was napping belowdecks. The shrew was literally starving, going on shorter rations than he'd ever remembered. He needed something to take his mind off the hunger.

So he straddled the steering mechanism on the top deck, testing to see if his leg was healed enough to turn the pedal and wind the engine. He winced with a tinge of pain every time he fully extended his left leg, but he found that he could in fact, with some effort, pilot the *Abigail*. So he did.

Archie started off cautiously enough. The houseboat was nowhere near as agile as his sea-cycle, but he possessed a natural instinct for boating and found piloting the *Abigail* to be nearly as easy as walking. Soon he was zipping and zagging along the waves. He hardly needed the telescope now. They were making good time towards safety; the sun warmed his skin, and the sea spray on his fur made him feel carefree. For a moment, Archie forgot how much trouble they were in.

And that's when the idea struck him. If he were to pull the brake and turn the *Abigail* hard at the peak of a wave, they ought to spin in a full circle as they rode down into the trough. It never occurred to the shrew that his idea might be dangerous. And he had no reason to do it except that it would further his understanding of how he might improve the performance and design of his invention. But once the idea had wedged itself in his brain, he thought about it almost as much as food.

The houseboat crested a medium roller. *That one would have been the perfect size!* His slender paws twitched at the controls, itching to try the maneuver. A small voice buzzed at the back of his mind telling him he ought not to attempt it, but Archie Shrew had become an expert at ignoring that voice.

He lasted two more waves and then came the perfect one. It was taller than most, casting a shadow over the *Abigail* as they approached. Slowly, they climbed up the rise of the wave. A school of menhaden darted to and fro beneath them, the small fish flashing sideways against the sun. White water crested gently at the peak, and for just a moment the scene resembled an oil painting of an old clipper ship, riding high atop the water, silhouetted against the sun, and reflecting the oranges, greens, and blues of the ocean and sky.

And then, unable to help himself, Archie pulled hard on both the brake and the steering levers. The *Abigail* lurched backward against the wave, tottered for just a moment, and fell. Archie laughed as the houseboat spun not once but in three complete circles into the trough. He released the brake at just the right time and the *Abigail* began chugging right up the rise of the next wave. The shrew chittered with excitement. Mr. Popli stirred belowdecks.

If Archie had stopped there, the disaster might have been a little less disaster-y. But the second wave looked as perfect as the first. The *Abigail* climbed slowly up the back side of the roller in the same way. The same fishes flashed against the sun and the houseboat tottered at the same gentle break at the crest. And Archie pulled with the same strength against the brake and the steering.

That's when two things happened that Archie could not have predicted. First, Mr. Popli had awakened from his nap and was climbing out of the hatch at the exact moment the *Abigail* began to spin. He slipped, clinging to the handle of the hatch as his houseboat circled down the wave.

Second, this particular wave contained a double

roller. A second, smaller wave had been overtaken by the larger one, making a steep shelf halfway down. If the *Abigail* had been plowing straight along, she might have powered over or been steered around the second wave. Instead, she tumbled over the edge like a toy falling off a table.

《 》

Mr. Popli gasped as he surfaced and began treading water. The *Abigail* lay on her side, no longer balanced— all the water barrels on the starboard side had been sheared off, as had the tarpaulin. The coil-powered engine continued to unwind, and the houseboat twisted in tight circles like an injured fish. He couldn't see Archie anywhere.

The next wave lifted Mr. Popli high above the *Abigail*, and he saw, to his horror, that the shrew floated facedown in the water, unmoving. What's more, with each second, Archie drifted closer and closer to the deadly churn of the paddle wheel.

Chug, chug, chug. The wheel shuddered against the water. Archie bobbed nearer still. *Chug, chug, chug.* It would smash him to pieces.

Swimming frantically, Mr. Popli called out to Archie. The paddle wheel now churned within a whisker of Archie's snout. Mr. Popli could not save him. He was too far away. He turned his head so he wouldn't see.

And then the engine clicked, the coil spring unwound, and the paddle wheel stopped.

Mr. Popli dove toward Archie. In that instant, the engine clicked again, turning the paddle wheel one last time. A wooden spoke from the wheel smacked Archie hard on his upper back, pushing the shrew beneath the surface.

Mr. Popli darted through the water toward Archie. Moments later, he was clinging to the side of the houseboat, squeaking to catch his breath. There was no time to rest. He inhaled deeply, starting in his lower belly and continuing up to his neck, using all his muscles to expand his chest and fill every fiber of his lungs. Kicking his legs up over his head, Mr. Popli dove headfirst into the deep.

Below the surface, an eerie calm overcame the mouse. His heart pulsed quickly for the first few beats and then slowed to match the steady undulations of the ocean. Finally, he spotted Archie. The shrew was sinking. Using his arms, legs, and tail to propel deeper, Mr. Popli chased him into the depths.

The school of menhaden swam circles around them, nipping harmlessly at the mouse and shrew, curious to see if anything tasty might fall from their fur. By the time Mr. Popli caught up with Archie, the *Abigail* was only a speck on the surface far above. He bit down on the shoulder strap of Archie's satchel and began dragging the shrew back to the surface.

A broad shadow swept across the mouse's field of vision. He shrieked underwater, letting go of Archie for a moment and losing precious air. But then the shadow was gone. Looking this way and that, he again pulled Archie toward the light. Halfway to the surface, Mr. Popli's chest began heaving. His lungs screamed for oxygen and his body desperately wanted him to take a breath. He fought the feeling and kicked harder.

Reaching toward the light, the mouse struggled for the surface but Archie's weight continued to pull against him.

Mr. Popli realized he couldn't save them both.

He let go of Archie.

Chapter 13

Before they could properly drown, Mr. Popli and Archie were almost slashed to pieces. Small fish bolted in all directions, crashing into the mammals. Behind them, an assailing swordfish thrashed its bill through the foaming water.

Fortunately, instead of mouse or shrew kabobs, the swordfish had a taste for the school of menhaden. As the fish swept past the duo, its powerful wake blasted them to the surface.

Open air triggered Archie's instinct to breathe. Mr. Popli gasped up beside him. He took another sputtering gulp of air and grabbed hold of Archie. They were still in terrible danger. *Out of the whirlpool and into the waterspout*, thought the mouse, dodging the fleeing fishes.

Archie coughed up water and began to take shallow breaths. Mr. Popli cradled him in his arms while treading water toward the *Abigail*. Meanwhile, the swordfish made a feast of the menhaden, its bill slashing violently just below the surface. The fish jumped every which way, crashing into Archie and Mr. Popli. At last, Mr. Popli reached the capsized houseboat, clinging to the open hatch with one paw and grasping Archie with his tail and other paw.

Bruised and scraped, missing fur and half-drowned, Mr. Popli managed to heave both of them through the hatch of the capsized *Abigail*. Barely conscious, Archie mumbled about snakes and eggs. *The egg!* thought Mr. Popli. *There's no way it could have survived. Merri would have been terribly disappointed.*

《 》

The mouse woke with his tongue stuck to the roof of his mouth. "Have a drink," came Archie's voice. A strong paw lifted his head. Something cool splashed against his teeth and he took a long draught. "Not too fast," said Archie. "You're dehydrated."

"What happened?"

"It was my fault," Archie confessed. "A giant wave came and I tried to pilot us through it. We got caught in a double roller." He left out the part about spinning the *Abigail* in circles for fun. It didn't feel like a lie. He'd told Mr. Popli all he needed to know, hadn't he?

"Did we lose sight of the island?"

"On the contrary," Archie said with a note of hope

in his voice. "We should be there tomorrow. And a good thing, too. You just drank the last of the unspoiled water."

Mr. Popli sat up slowly in his bunk. From whiskers to tail, his entire body ached as though he'd been chewed up and spit out. The *Abigail* floated upright. A cool wind blew into the hatch, but the sun quickly warmed it through the translucent plastic hull of the ship. "How did you get us upright?"

"It was easy." Archie shrugged. "We'd lost all of the starboard ballast. So I cut loose the water barrels on the port side, and after I bailed all the water that seeped in through the vents, we flipped right back up. The biggest challenge was what to do with you. In the end I had to roll you into a corner and tie you down so you wouldn't go flying."

Mr. Popli groaned, noticing the rope burns on his wrists. Archie continued. "The *Abigail* is quite a vessel. She's still perfectly functional and locomotive. I gathered the port water barrels and reattached two on each side so we're balanced again. Even if they're filled with salt water."

"And the egg?"

"You wouldn't believe it, but it's perfectly fine! When we wrapped it in those blankets and stowed it away before the storm, we couldn't have made it any safer. What's more, it's almost ready to hatch!"

Gingerly, Mr. Popli sat up in his bunk. "I can't believe all you've done! How long was I asleep?"

"I don't know. You were unconscious when I woke up. It's been half a day since then."

"But we're nearly home?! Archie, it's a miracle. You've saved us both. You're a hero."

Archie offered the mouse a lopsided grin and turned away. He knew that his curiosity had put them in danger in the first place. He wanted to tell Mr. Popli the whole story, but he couldn't make the words form in his mouth. He didn't feel like a hero at all.

Perhaps now I can be, though, he told himself. *If Mr. Popli thinks I'm a hero, he'll tell all of the citizens, and they'll think I am, too. This time, things will be different. I'll be a new shrew. No more lies, no more mistakes. I'll triple-test all of my inventions before showing them to anyone. No one will get hurt because of Archie Shrew ever again.*

Archie's promise lasted nearly a whole day.

Chapter 14

Enchanted by the sight of the island, the duo ignored any signs of danger. Mr. Popli looked through the telescope, then handed it back to Archie. "We must be coming around to a part of the badlands we haven't properly explored," said the mouse. "I don't recognize a thing—not even the wall."

"We'll have to make land anyway," said Archie. "We haven't got a drop of water left. And you haven't eaten in days." Mr. Popli had given up the last of the rations to Archie. A mouse, as Mr. Popli put it, could better weather the storms of hunger.

They steered the *Abigail* into the outstretched arms of a shallow cove. An enormous upside-down wooden boat protected the cove on one side, surrounded by an amalgamation of plastic bags, bottles, and bits of dangerous-looking jagged metal. On the other side, a wooden totem pole jutted out from the debris, its carven faces scowling at the sky. Sun-bleached rubber ducks bobbed silently amidst the flotsam.

The duo became suddenly aware of just how much noise they made. Clicks from the engine and the splash of the paddle wheel reverberated off the walls of trash. No sounds of life responded.

If the strange quiet made the two nervous, the odor unsettled them further. The citizens of Garbage Island had worked hard to clear away rot and decay. With all they'd built and planted, their island had a rich aroma, almost earthy. It smelled of sawdust and salt water, campfires and frying fish. It smelled like home. The air here smelled unfamiliar, sickly sweet.

Archie and Mr. Popli exchanged nervous glances. "This isn't our island," said Archie at last.

"You're right," the mouse agreed. "But we need water. And food. We need string and boards and barrels to repair the *Abigail*. We don't know what's out there, but we need to explore. And you need a weapon."

Archie nodded, raising a bushy eyebrow. "I've got a few ideas."

《 》

As the *Abigail* chugged deeper into the cove, Mr. Popli grew more nervous at the prospect of exploring an unknown island. But anticipation of a different sort took root in the back of Archie's mind. If this was the first island that they'd found, maybe his family had discovered it as well! Maybe they'd succeeded in turning this island of flotsam into a shrew paradise. Maybe he was a whisker away from home!

Mr. Popli pulled the brake lever to stop the engine. Archie leapt onto the totem pole, lashing the *Abigail*'s mooring line around the protruding stub of a wooden eagle beak. Thousands of eyes watched their arrival from the shadows. Venomous drool slid down fangs. Stomachs murmured hungrily.

The duo checked on the egg, gathered their weapons, and set off. Mr. Popli held his glass knife in his left paw, putting it between his teeth whenever they had to climb a particularly difficult section of garbage. They needed fresh water more than anything, and the cleanest water would be found higher up, collected in pools made by plastic bags and in glass bottles turned just the right way toward the sky.

If we don't find water today, thought the mouse, *it may be the end of this whole pitiful adventure.* He felt sorry for his home, for the citizens he'd failed to protect. He wondered how long the islanders would survive if he didn't make it back.

Beside him, the shrew struggled to shift the contraption strapped across his back. It was clever, Mr. Popli had to admit. A long spear of wood, whittled sharp at one end, could be used to defend against

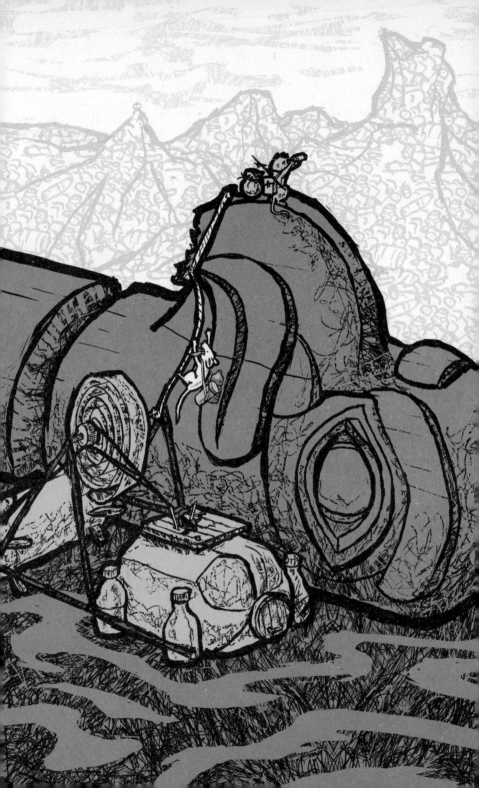

enemies that got too close. But Archie had modified the spear with a small crossbeam topped with a plastic circlet about a third of the way down. This allowed him to attach a rubber band to the crossbeam and track arrows through the circlet. It was something between a crossbow and a slingshot—accurate and powerful. A quiver of toothpick-sized arrows hung alongside it.

Each of them carried empty containers for fresh water, but Archie couldn't resist stuffing his satchel with every interesting thing he found along the way. He was weighed down with sharp shards of glass for arrowheads, perfectly round beads for bearings, and paper clips that could be bent into any shape. He had also found a rare box of waterproof matches that he'd dragged, heaving, all the way to the peak of the mound they were climbing.

Archie dropped his treasures, took a long draught from the pool, and immediately spat it out.

"It tastes like oil. Poisoned."

"Snakespit."

Their throats ached from lack of water.

Archie gnawed on an arrow from his quiver. Mr. Popli gave him a sideways look.

"What? I have to eat something."

Mr. Popli pointed at a shimmer on the horizon. "That might be another pool over there."

From his satchel, Archie retrieved the looking glass and, after peering through it for a minute, handed it to Mr. Popli.

"It does look like a pool," said the mouse, still staring through the glass. "Though it will take the rest of the morning to get there, and we'll be lucky to be back at the *Abigail* by dark. And Archibald!" he said, jumping straight up. "There's something moving along the edge."

"What is it? Let me see!"

He handed Archie the looking glass. "I don't see it. What did it look like?"

"I don't know. It was like a tiny cloud of shadow. Riding on a blur."

"Nothing like . . . a shrew?"

Mr. Popli took Archie's meaning. "I don't know, Archibald. I don't think so. This doesn't seem like a hospitable place for shrews or mice."

"Oh," was all Archie could reply.

They left most of what Archie had gathered at the base of the first mound, which they named Graywater, because of the tainted pool at the top. With less to carry, they scurried across the terrain, moving stealthily from nook to cranny, paws never far from their weapons.

Every bobbing bit of flotsam, every skittering shadow seemed like an invisible enemy. Even Archie began to lose hope of seeing a long-lost cousin. He would not have wished them the bad luck of trying to survive on this desolate terrain. Still, nothing openly impeded their progress. They reached the second pool by high noon.

"Is the water good?" Mr. Popli asked, his back to the pool, his long knife clutched in both paws.

"It is!" said Archie, taking another long draught. The pair took turns, one drinking and filling bottles while the other stood guard. There was no sign of the figure Mr. Popli had seen skirting along the shore. But he thought he saw shadows in the distance, and there seemed to be a trail through the debris.

A patch of dandelions bloomed near the fresh water, and they feasted on the seeds, collecting the stems to begin resupplying the *Abigail*. Although it was a good meal, they needed much more. Mr. Popli had thinned on their voyage, but Archie had grown so skinny that he could easily count his ribs. Stress and hunger had caused the shrew to lose patches of fur, and he had a new, empty gleam in his eyes.

Weighed down with water, Mr. Popli decided they should come back for Archie's treasures the next day. Archie protested. "But what if that blurry figure you saw comes and takes them in the night?"

"Nothing we found had been hidden. It was all in

plain sight. I can only deduce that, whatever I saw, it isn't a builder like us. It's a scavenger."

"All the more reason to get out of here quickly! Let's take our things and get back to the ship. Maybe tomorrow we can navigate to the other side of the island and see if things are different."

"We still need more food. And repairs. I've seen plenty that we can use here. Whatever that thing was, it didn't look big enough to do us any harm. We'll be safe."

As soon as they made it back to the houseboat, they collapsed into their bunks.

Archie was disappointed by the lack of evidence that a family of shrews might have landed here, but he tried to put on a brave face. "Some adventure, wouldn't you say, Mr. Popli?"

"No, not particularly."

"But we've survived against all odds!"

"I suppose."

"Oh, come now, tomorrow's a new day. What's the worst that could happen?"

But Mr. Popli had already fallen asleep. And Archie soon did, too, completely unaware of the creatures gathering around their boat.

Chapter 15

Archie's curiosity saved their lives that night, but not without consequences. He'd woken hours before dawn, unable to stop thinking of the treasures he'd left at the foot of the Graywater mound. Mr. Popli snored like a walrus.

It would only take a few shakes of a shrew's tail to go and get them. And I'm wide awake anyhow. And so Archie did what he usually did. Ignoring the small voice in the back of his head, he snuck past the sleeping Mr. Popli and right into the spiders' trap.

They did not expect Archie to come alone. And although they outnumbered him a hundred to one, none of the small spiders wanted to openly attack the shrew. The shrew had a weapon and he was bigger than any of them except their queen. So they waited as he clumsily crossed their garbage patch by moonlight. They watched as he drew near to his left-behind treasure trove. And they giggled excitedly as Archie tripped and fell into the sticky web they'd woven all over the ground.

Archie didn't know what he'd fallen in, only that it was clingy and tangly. He struggled against it, growing more and more stuck as he tried to free himself. By the time he'd finished rolling around in the webbing, Archie could barely move. The spiders didn't even need to restrain him with venom to bring him back to their lair. He was a neat and tidy package.

The spiders trekked expertly across the garbage patch by moonlight, passing Archie back and forth when they climbed difficult terrain. With a silk rope, they pulled him up the side of a rogue weather buoy entangled with fishing nets.

Immobilized, hanging upside down, being dragged toward his death by a spider army, Archie began to question his decisions. *Perhaps I should have waited till morning and gone out with Mr. Popli. At the very least I ought to have left a note.*

An itchy spot throbbed just below Archie's knee. Bound as he was, he couldn't scratch it. The momentary irritation became almost worse than his fear of what lay ahead. He cleared his throat to ask the spiders to let him scratch. But at that moment the spiders' city emerged over the horizon, glistening against the rising sun. Archie forgot about his itch, and his eyes grew as big as bottle caps. *They're not scavengers at all*, he marveled. *They're builders.*

Stretching as far as the shrew could see, the garbage had been transformed into a sweeping city. Spiraling towers reached toward the clouds. Intricate roads and bridges crisscrossed the skyline. Enormous wind catchers twisted in the early morning breeze. Thick ropes ran at angles along the roads and bridges, though it wasn't immediately clear what they were used for. And everything was made of silk! The base of the island was still familiar debris, but the higher he looked, the more beautiful structures he saw.

The spiders carried their prisoner through the city. Sometimes climbing, sometimes completely upside down, they used their hooked claws to pull themselves along the woven paths.

Archie might have shuddered to see the thousands of cocooned pods scattered below the roadways containing the remains of the spiders' unfortunate victims. He could have worried about what it would feel like to have his insides liquefied by deadly venom. Instead, Archie mused at all the creative ways in which the spiders had used their different types of silk.

Undulating spirals of silk funneled beads of dew into cisterns. Dry, heavy silk ropes anchored buildings and bridges to the debris. Fields of thin, wispy silk stretched out in the wind like tentacles, snatching at anything that flew too close. But what impressed Archie the most was how the spiders had combined the different types of silk to create new things.

Clusters of heavy silk had been entwined with sticky patches to create supports for buildings. Fisherspiders used lines of fine gossamer silk to lure small fish into inescapable underwater nets. Layers of interwoven silk types baked in the sun and hardened into structural walls for buildings that seemed, to Archie, more beautiful than terrifying. He instantly catalogued thirty-seven ways he could use the spider silk back on his island. *Just as soon as Mr. Popli gets here to rescue me, which should be any moment.*

<< >>

"You'll never get me to leave this ship!"

A spider leg clawed at Mr. Popli through the porthole as he slammed the hatch shut. The appendage fell, still twitching, onto the mid deck. Instinctively, the mouse picked it up and put it in his mouth. *This is bad. This is very bad. Well, the situation is bad. This*—he chewed the spider leg thoughtfully—*is quite good, actually.*

Spider warriors lined the shore and perched atop the houseboat, now anchored to the island by ropes of strong web. The spiders had no way of getting in, but

123

the boat could not leave. Not that he would attempt an escape without knowing what had happened to Archie. *If only that pestiferous shrew had left a note!*

Mr. Popli considered his current circumstance, and it was precarious at best. He had some food—in fact he'd spent the morning twilight chiseling fat barnacles from the totem pole, thinking of what he'd say to Archie when the shrew finally turned up. But then the spiders had come. Now, without knowing Archie's fate, he loathed the idea of trying to leave the island. And with most of the fresh water stored outside the hull, he could only hold out so long. He knew it, and so did the spiders.

"WE HAS YOU FRIEND!" The spider language differed from the dialect they spoke on Garbage Island, but Mr. Popli understood the threat perfectly.

"Well, then give him back!" he called through a vent, refusing to open the hatch. "And then we'll leave you in peace!"

"COME OUT!"

"Why?"

"SO WE CAN EAT—OW!"

The sound of scuffling ended with the voice of a different spider. "WE TAKE YOU TO YOU FRIEND. HIM HURT."

"What was that part about eating something or someone?"

"NOTHING!"

"I don't believe you! Bring Archibald here! I won't come out till I hear his voice."

"OKAY." More scuffling sounds along with the whispering of spiders.

"THIS IS ARCH-EEEY-BAAALD. COME OUT NOW, MOUSE."

"That's a terrible impersonation!"

"THIS HIM. PROMISE. SQUEEEEAAAAK."

"It sounds nothing like him! And he doesn't squeak; it's more of a chitter. Bring him here or I'll just starve to death in this houseboat and you'll never get to eat me."

"OKAY. WE COME BACK. BRING FRIEND. AND QUEENY."

Chapter 16

The spiders deposited Archie in the city center, in a courtyard made of hardened silk pavers. He could balance on his haunches but remained otherwise immobile because of the sticky web binding him. Winding columns twisted toward the sky. More heavy silk ropes stretched into nearby towers.

Archie wondered why the spiders had scurried away so hastily. *It's not as if anything could sneak up on you here.*

There was a zipping, whooshing rush behind him. He felt a sudden presence. A shadow. The click of metal on paver. Hopping on immobilized feet, he turned and beheld the spider queen.

A crown sat on her head. The head was impaled on a pike. The pike extended from the paw of the biggest rat Archie had ever seen.

Standing three shrews tall, the rat was missing a hind paw and part of her tail. A false paw made of brass nails and wire was attached to her leg with spider webbing. The last several inches of her tail had been rebuilt using lengths of fishing line wrapped round with silk. A small gold hook dangled from the end of her braided tail. It whipped back and forth as she studied Archie.

"Nasty business, the sticky web." Her voice was sugary sweet, but with a hint of underlying venom.

"Do you think you could let me out? I'm getting a bit of a cramp."

"I try not to touch the stuff. I'm afraid I might get stuck in it as well," she said. "Who are you? And why are you here?"

"Well, I'm Archie—er—Archibald. I'm a shrew. A very sore and hungry one at that. Do you know many shrews?" he asked hopefully.

"You are the first I've ever met, friend shrew."

Her response strengthened his notion that his family had not made it to this island. But at least she'd called him *friend*. Perhaps he'd get out of this without losing his skin. "I'd be glad for a friend right about now. For a moment I thought I was about to be eaten."

"Oh, I've eaten many a friend," said the hulking rat.

Archie chittered nervously as his self-defense odor filled the air around him.

"But I've yet to decide about you," the rat continued.

"You're a bit scrawny and you stink. Again I'll ask, why are you here on my island?"

Her island? Who exactly is this rat?

"I'd be happy to tell you my story, good lady. But may I ask precisely whom I am addressing?"

"You address royalty. I am the Spider Queen. At least I have been"—she gestured toward the head on the end of her pike—"since the previous leader stepped down."

Archie gulped. "Your Majesty." He tried to bow, but, still tangled in the spider web, he nearly flopped onto his face instead. Steadying himself, he asked, "Are you sure there's no way you might get me out of this webbing? And I wouldn't say no to some barnacle bread or a crab-cake sandwich. If you have any, that is." *If I am going to die, I'd hate to do it on an empty stomach.*

"Both reasonable requests." She stomped her metal foot on the pavers. "Refreshments! For . . . my friend." Spiders scurried in the corners of Archie's vision.

The rat flashed a dagger-sharp set of teeth at the shrew, more grimace than smile.

She's definitely going to eat me. Unless I can invent a way out of this mess. Think, Archie, think!

"The secret to getting loose from sticky web is oil,"

the rat continued. "And oil is rather rare, which is why I stay away from the webbing at all costs."

"Oh, I see. I suppose I'll need to be off to go find some." He took a tentative hop toward the open end of the courtyard.

"Goodness, no!" She scrambled between Archie and the exit, moving faster on the false foot than Archie would have thought possible. "I wouldn't dream of leaving in your state. The spiders will think I've set you free."

"Is that bad?"

"Exceptionally. If I let you go, they'll think *they* get to eat you. I'm afraid once you've made it this far inside the island the chances of not being eaten are relatively small."

"That *is* bad."

The rat leaned in furtively. "Now listen, I've got some oil that I keep for emergencies. But I'd hate to waste it on someone I intend to eat. So if I were you, I'd try to convince me that you're more useful alive."

"And how might I do that?"

"My friends used to tell me the best stories," she mused. "But I haven't had one in some time. Tell me a story, Archibald."

"A story?"

"*Your* story. Make it dramatic! And desperate!

Those are my favorite kinds of tales. Make it good and perhaps I'll get you out of the sticky web."

"And off your island?"

"That depends."

"On what?"

"On how good a storyteller you are. So, will you attempt to entertain me with your unbelievable tale?"

That should be easy, thought Archie. *There's nothing less believable than the truth.*

"I accept, but it will be rather difficult, wrapped up as I am. I'm one of those shrews who likes to use his paws when telling a story. You'd miss out on the drama."

"You'd run away."

"I wouldn't! Shrew's honor." He crossed his fingers as he said it.

"Did you cross your fingers?"

"No!" Archie crossed the digits on his other paw as he told a second lie.

"Very well, then. But if you're lying, I get to eat you."

"Agreed." He tried to cross his toes, but they were stuck together.

From somewhere in her rolling, matted fur, the Spider Queen Who Was Actually a Rat produced a vial. As the rat dripped tiny beads of oil from her claws onto the shrew, Archie squirmed out of the sticky web. He marveled at how easily it came loose once the oil ran down his fur.

The queen recoiled when she saw the arrow launcher still strapped to his back.

"Oh, this? Please don't worry, Your Majesty. It's not loaded or anything."

"Will you set it down? It frightens me." He did. She stepped between Archie and his weapon, casually kicking it backward.

Not that I could fight my way out of this mess in any case. She'd flay me open with one of those wicked claws before I could spit. Free of the web, Archie stretched and preened, more for show than anything else. It did little to improve his ragged appearance.

But then the refreshments came—fish eyes, sea horse livers, and a tiny plastic bottle filled with fresh water. All of it descended from the top of a nearby column wrapped in silk. *The spiders won't come anywhere near her. Probably better for their health. But why don't they trap her the way they did me?*

Archie ate and drank ravenously. He finished off the last eyeball with an inelegant burp.

"I've given you food and drink and freed you from your bonds," said the queen. "And now I expect a tantalizing tale in return."

Archie rose to stand before her in a formal sort of way. He tried to look past her toward his arrow launcher, but her girth hid the exact location of his weapon. "My lady," Archie began, bowing all the way to the ground. "We are wayfarers lost at sea! Realizing we have trespassed on your island, we beg your forgiveness. But had we not made land, we certainly would have been, um, most horribly wrenched from this life into, er, Poseidon's Boneyard."

"We?" the rat interrupted. "How many of you are there?"

"There are two of us, Your Majesty. Well, three, if you count the egg."

"Two of you and an egg." She sounded disappointed. "That's not very many. And what manner of animals are your companions?"

"Mr. Popli is a mouse. And the egg is, well, an egg."

"Yes, well, forgive me. Now pray, continue your story. But tell me how it began! When did you set out? And from where?"

"Of course, my lady."

And so Archie, thinking more about his escape than his words, began to tell his story truthfully. He didn't notice her eyes gleam when he mentioned the hundreds of small, edible animals on his island. Nor did he see her tail quiver with excitement, right down to the gold hook, when he detailed their storehouses filled with food and the exact defenses designed to protect them.

It was only when he'd finished describing precisely how he'd gotten in and out through his secret entrance in order to rescue the egg, and the rat queen whipped her tail triumphantly, that Archie realized his mistake. He'd just betrayed his island to a rat queen with an army of spiders, who could now sneak past the wall, through his secret door, and into an unsuspecting community filled with his friends and neighbors.

"So which way do you spin the board to open the secret door?" the rat questioned. "Just out of curiosity."

Snakespit. "Um . . . Up?"

"And I suppose if up failed to work then one would try down."

Double snakespit!

"But what else can you tell me about your journey? How long have you been at sea? From which direction did you come?"

"Oh, um. East. I think. Or was it west?"

"Which was it?" Her fur bristled impatiently. The edges of her snout curled into a snarl.

Think, Archie, think! "I forgot to tell you the most important part!" he blurted. "We have a snake! Her name is Colubra. Mr. Popli tells her what to do. When he whistles for her, she comes as fast as a tuna. And she's as big around as an eel!"

The rat queen grimaced. "Really? As fast as a tuna? As big as an eel? And this Mr. Popli commands her? The one that's here on my island with you?"

"Y-y-yes," stammered Archie. All the hairs on his back tingled with alarm. The rat's tail swished with delight, the gold hook clinking against the courtyard pavers.

"I wonder if *he* remembers where you left your island."

A trembling spider approached, having apparently drawn the short straw. The rat leaned down so the spider could whisper in her ear. She nodded, a smile spreading. Her thick, hairless tail undulated back and forth like a shark on the hunt. Message delivered, the spider began to slink away. She snapped her jaws. The spider jumped and scurried backward. She winked at Archie as if they were sharing a joke. Then, with a flick of her tail, she impaled the retreating spider on her golden hook and swung it into her mouth. *Snap. Chomp. Swallow.* It was gone.

"Thank you for such a fascinating story, Archibald Shrew. As it turns out, your Mr. Popli wants to meet me as much as I'd like to meet him." With an impressive leap, she whipped her tail up and over one of the thick

135

ropes stretched tightly across the courtyard. The hook caught the rope and the queen rode it like a zip line from one end of the courtyard toward the other. Halfway across, she swung herself up and flicked her tail again, catching a different rope and zipping back to where Archie stood, awed by the simple genius of her invention.

"So that's how you get around without getting caught in sticky web!" said the shrew. He then remembered all of the ropes stretched across the city. *Fascinating!*

"Just who are you?" he wondered out loud.

"I doubt you really want to know." And with that, she lifted Archie with one paw, tucked him under her arm, and leapt up to the nearest line. A moment later, they were zipping above the city toward the coast.

Chapter 17

The spiders skidded and stumbled over one another in their rush to get out of the queen's way. News traveled fast when she was particularly hungry. Or angry. Or when her tea arrived tepid. Honestly, the smarter spiders kept a permanent distance. Natural selection took care of the rest.

With an acrobatic flip, the rat landed on the totem pole to which the *Abigail* was tethered. She deposited Archie in front of her and dug thornlike claws into the nape of his neck. She nudged him to speak. When he hesitated, she tightened her grip.

"H-hello, Mr. Popli! I'm here!" Archie called.

"Archibald?"

"Yes! It's me!"

"Is it safe to come out?"

"I should think not! No, not even a little!" The rat twisted her claw. Archie whined.

"Mr. Popli, is it?" said the Spider Queen.

"Yes, and who are you?"

"I rule this island, which you have trespassed on and ransacked."

"Completely unintentional, I assure you. I don't suppose you'd be satisfied with a sincere apology?"

"I will promise you safe passage," said the rat. "But as for the return of your friend, we'll need to negotiate."

"Then perhaps we ought to discuss this over tea. Will you come aboard?"

"I'd never fit. But I will invite you ashore and promise your safety. For now. My palace is not too far."

"I'm not sure I'm willing to leave my ship," Mr. Popli called back. "And heading inland sounds like a wonderful way to end up as someone's dinner."

"It is!" Archie yipped as the queen twisted a claw into the tender part of his back.

"Then I suppose we're through here," said the queen. "Say good-bye to your friend."

"Good-bye, Archibald!"

"Mr. Popli?" Archie never imagined the mouse would leave him to die. After all they'd been through, he'd begun to think of Mr. Popli as a friend.

"Just kidding. I'm coming out. But I insist we make space to picnic on the shore. Otherwise our tea will get cold."

"I do hate cold tea." The queen agreed.

Minutes later, on a silk picnic blanket draped across the totem pole, the three mammals sat sipping tea like old friends. More food had been brought by the spiders. Mr. Popli carefully chewed a bit of pickled mackerel kidney. Across from the mouse, Archie appeared small and frightened, seated before the hulking rat. An army of spiders skulked in the surrounding garbage cliffs.

The *Abigail* listed against the strong web ropes that held her firmly in place two rat lengths away. Small bait fish darted to and fro near the water's surface— almost as if they sensed a meal about to be served and hoped they might have a chance at the table scraps.

If it surprised Mr. Popli to discover a giant rat as the queen of the spiders, he hid it convincingly. "My queen, how are you enjoying the dandelion tea? The secret is to squeeze in a drop of barnacle juice just as it's steeping. How fortunate that you had all the ingredients right here on your island."

The queen, for her part, eyed Mr. Popli uncertainly. She ruled with fear and guile and savagery—but this mouse seemed intelligent and unafraid, yet savage in his own way.

"Unusual," she said. "Delicious. But stolen waters are sweet."

"So they are," the mouse confessed. "And so it seems we must beg for your mercy. But I am curious, how precisely did we come to steal from you? It seems . . . unusual that a figure such as yourself would command a host of carnivorous predators. To be more direct, why haven't the spiders eaten you?"

"Oh, they tried. When I stumbled onto this island seven moons ago, I was as skinny as you are. And wounded. I got caught in the spiders' sticky web. They thought I would make an excellent meal. They had no idea of my . . . hunger . . . to survive." She smiled maliciously.

"They came with ten warriors. A snack. They attacked me with twenty. I ate them all. And then they wouldn't come close anymore. They hid in the shadows, taunting me, waiting till I fell asleep or passed out. But I wouldn't. And when the previous queen came to investigate, I chose that moment to free myself from my bonds." She flashed her teeth and chomped menacingly, then jingled her brass foot and swished her tail. "The old queen had a sweet flavor, like caramel."

Mr. Popli shivered. "It sounds as though our histories are similar. We came to this island lost and in need of help, just like you. We were trapped by the spiders as you were. Perhaps you can see yourself in our story and find a way to pardon us for this unintentional trespass."

"Don't forget attempted thievery." She indicated a silk bag overflowing with the treasures Archie had collected. He stared at it and thought mournfully of his arrow launcher, lost forever back in the queen's lair.

"If you can see us safely away, we'd be happy to compensate you." Mr. Popli had brought out all the valuable objects he owned. His knife, blankets, various inventions—anything useful was spread out as an offering to the queen.

The rat picked up each of the items in turn. She considered a contraption made of rubber bands and paper clips, then flipped it over her shoulder into the ocean.

"Hey!" said Archie. "That was my bottle cap shooter!"

"Your trinkets don't interest me."

"It was very helpful." Archie sulked.

"But I understand you have an egg. I haven't had an egg in ages."

Mr. Popli looked startled for the first time and glanced sharply at the shrew. Archie stared guiltily down into his lap. "The egg is a member of our crew and as such is protected by your promise of safety."

"That's an unfortunate interpretation of my promise," said the queen.

What is this game they play? thought Archie. *She*

could have all of us to eat, including the egg, anytime she wants. And Mr. Popli can do nothing to stop her.

"What else could you offer me?" said the queen. "Stories? I've heard all about your wonderful island with its ingenious wall. But what about your journey? From which direction did you come? How many days did it take to get here?" Her hooked tail swished excitedly.

Mr. Popli's brow furrowed and he twitched his whiskers. He began peeling off bits of pickled kidney and whipping them right at Archie's snout.

"Why—"

"Ouch!"

"Archibald—"

"Stop it!"

"Would you tell this rat—"

"That hurts!"

"ABOUT OUR ISLAND?!"

The rat laughed, her tail swishing faster than ever. Archie, for his part, was terribly confused. He'd seen Mr. Popli angry, but never like this. *In our all years he's never thrown things at me. And he'd never waste food. It makes no sense!*

"You've got us cornered," said Mr. Popli at last. "I'll give you the egg in exchange for Archie, but we'll never lead you to our island."

144

"NO!" shouted Archie, ducking as another projectile sailed past his ear and down the side of the totem pole.

"No," said the rat. "I thought you might lead me to an island full of new delicacies. But now you're better off as a large meal I'll need to sleep off. My army will find your island in time."

Archie quailed. This was all his fault. First he'd gotten them into this mess, and then he'd betrayed his entire island to the rat queen and her spider army.

Mr. Popli, however, did not flinch his fur. "Then I'm afraid we must leave you unsatisfied. Archibald, get up. It's time for us to go." He stood and turned his back to the hulking rat.

The queen leapt up in a rage, ready to whip at Mr. Popli with her tail hook. Unfortunately for her, the hook was occupied. A piece of kidney that had flown over Archie's right ear had impaled itself on the rat's hook. Her tail, swishing in and out of the water, had attracted one of the small fish. Unbeknownst to the rat, that small fish had both the kidney and the hook in its mouth.

When the queen tried to raise her tail to slash at Mr. Popli, the fish began fighting. Flopping to and fro underwater, it unbalanced the queen. She stumbled sideways. Her false foot slipped on the totem pole.

Digging in with her remaining back claw, she grabbed hold of her tail and tugged against the persistent fish. But a rather large fish, a wahoo, had noticed the smaller, flailing fish and raced up from the depths to investigate. There was a crash, a splash, a squeal; and thus ended the seven-month reign of the rat queen of the spiders. No one ever even found out her real name, but the wahoo thought she tasted like caramel.

Chapter 18

"Archibald, the spiders!" Surprised by the sudden kerplopping of their queen, the spiders had taken a moment to gape at the empty space where she had just been. Now they stalked the duo in careful steps.

"Don't worry! I've got this under control." Archie addressed the advancing horde using the dialect he'd heard them speak as they carried him to their city.

"HELLO, SPIDERS. ME ARCHIE. ME BEAT OLD QUEEN. ME NEW KING!"

This caused them to stop and consider, but only for a moment.

"WE HAVE KING," announced a spider.

"FOR DINNER!" another added. Spider cheers rose from the garbage. Their advance resumed in creeps and sprints.

"Forget what I said, Mr. Popli! We should definitely be going!"

Mr. Popli was already heaving the silk bag, now stuffed with their own possessions as well as Archie's treasures, back toward the *Abigail*.

Archie wrenched a long splinter from the totem pole and wielded it like a spear. Spiders halted in their tracks wherever he slashed, but for every one that stopped, ten advanced.

Mr. Popli shoved the bag in through the hatch, then clambered up the side of the ship. With his glass knife, he hacked at the webbing that held the houseboat in place. He sliced through five, then six of the ropes. The first of the spiders leapt onto the *Abigail*, launching itself at Mr. Popli. He stabbed at it with his knife. It fell. Two more had already landed. One curled up with Archie's makeshift spear in its side, but the other was scuttling toward them, and still more were leaping for the ship. The shrew launched himself through the porthole. Mr. Popli dove in behind him and slammed the hatch.

"Archibald," said Mr. Popli.

"Yes?"

"Didn't I suggest that we install the steering mechanism on the *inside*?"

"Yes. Yes, you did."

"Is it okay if I choose this moment to say *I told you so*?"

"Only if it makes you feel better about our up-coming death."

"I think it might."

"Then by all means, go ahead."

"I told you so."

« »

It was so dark inside the *Abigail* it might have been midnight, if midnight skittered and thumped and swore. The spiders threw themselves recklessly on the houseboat, coating it in layers of crawling shadow. Mr. Popli and Archie, as usual, argued over what to do next.

"We're at a stalemate. They can't get in. We can't get out," said Mr. Popli. "If we wait long enough, they may eventually leave."

"Or come back with some new and terrible invention designed to skewer houseboats, mice, and shrews all in one stroke."

"Then I would certainly welcome any brilliant ideas you might have!"

"And I would be glad to offer them!" Archie retorted. "As soon as I have one."

The spiders' idea came first.

"What's happening?!" asked Archie, gripping a rope as the entire houseboat listed to one side.

"We're going up!" said Mr. Popli. "They're pulling the whole boat inland!"

"No. It's worse," said the shrew, peering through a vent. "I think in fact they are going to skewer us. On *that*."

Along the water, near the fishing nets, a metal spike shot up, jagged and rusting in the sun. Tall and narrow, it glistened with bits of hardened webbing that gave it a sinister beauty. At its base, a large basin revealed the serrated rib cage of a fish far too big to be overcome by even a small army of spiders.

Mr. Popli joined Archie at the vent. The spiders had constructed a crane out of broomsticks and paint stirrers and even an old fishing rod, all held together by webbing. The crane stretched out over the spike like an arm bent at an impossible angle. A silk rope attached to the houseboat ran through the crane's eyelets. Little by little, the spiders were tugging the crew over the garbage toward the spike.

"So you think they're going to pull us up above that spike and then drop the whole houseboat?" Mr. Popli asked.

"Yes! It's rather brilliant, actually. We should think about making one. We could have fish for weeks!"

"Except that we're about to be skewered and then eaten by spiders. Remember?"

"Excellent point, Mr. Popli. Unless . . ."

"If you have an idea, Archibald, now would be a perfectly appropriate time to share it." The *Abigail* bumped over a floating log, tossing the animals inside the hull. Archie shot a worried look toward the egg, still stowed tightly away. Spiders skittered and fell from the top deck.

"Well, look there. They've got to pull us up over that barrel. We might be able to cut the line when we're halfway up and fall right into that canal toward open water. That's *if* the spiders don't attack us right away *and* we cut the rope at the precise moment *and* the boat lands pointed in the right direction. We'd have a straight shot out to sea. Then we'd be off for home!"

"So you're saying that we'll most likely be skewered and eaten?"

"Yes."

But since no better plans presented themselves, Archie and Mr. Popli agreed to give it a try. When they felt the houseboat clang against the side of the barrel, Mr. Popli reached to release the lock on the hatch. But then he paused for a moment, turned toward Archie, and extended a paw. "I'm sorry I've always been so cross with you. I only ever wanted to keep everyone safe."

Speechless at Mr. Popli's apology, Archie could only nod back in reply. The two grasped paws as friends and rushed out together.

The spiders were waiting.

Mr. Popli slashed with his long knife, and Archie attacked with the only weapon he could find, his telescope. In the face of this onslaught, spiders slipped and slid across the surface of the rocking *Abigail*, splashing into the water below.

And then Archie did something very brave and very stupid. From a position of relative safety, he vaulted right into the center of a ring of spiders protecting the rope. He poked at eyes and clubbed at legs. The spiders retreated—but only a whisker's length.

"I'm stuck!" he shouted to Mr. Popli, who was busy fighting off spiders of his own. Mr. Popli crashed into the nearest spider before scrambling toward Archie. He felt a pinch on his shoulder and spun around, hacking at the spider behind him.

And then Mr. Popli was inside the ring of spiders with the shrew. "Don't come any closer!" shouted Archie between parries with the spiders. "They've laid sticky web all around. You'll have to throw me your knife so I can cut us down."

Tossing the knife toward Archie's outstretched paw, Mr. Popli bared his teeth and extended his claws toward the rush of spiders. A hiss erupted in his throat and he charged the spiders, a blur of crunching and squishing and tearing.

Suddenly they were falling. Mr. Popli leapt for the

steering mechanism and clung to it. Spiders filled the air—some sliding off, some jumping from higher up, trying to recapture their prey.

But it was too late for the spider clan. The *Abigail* splashed down. At the helm, Mr. Popli pedaled for all he was worth. Spiders churned in the houseboat's wake. Archie shook his tail at the final pursuers, who, too slow to overtake them, had given up.

The less injured spiders who could still walk on water scurried away back toward the island. Archie noted, curiously, that any spiders who fell underwater or were splashed by the salt spray quickly curled up and twitched as if in excruciating pain.

The shrew finished hewing his way through the sticky web on the *Abigail*'s roof.

Mr. Popli reached toward the pinch on his shoulder and recognized the shape and tender sting of a spider bite. He stopped pedaling.

"I have to admit," said Archie. "I wasn't sure we were going to survive that one."

"I was thinking the same thing," Mr. Popli said just before he collapsed, rolling into the ocean.

《 》

Archie dove into the cool water after the mouse. He heaved the limp body up the water barrels, through the hatch, and inside the houseboat.

"Mr. Popli! Wake up!" He slapped the mouse on the nose, yanked hard on his tail, and twisted his left ear. It was only when he poked the mouse right in the spider bite that Mr. Popli's eyes flashed open and he shot up, howling.

Archie helped the mouse to his bunk and covered him with a blanket. He checked on the egg. He nibbled a dead spider. Then he climbed back up to the helm.

This is some mess you've gotten yourself into, Archie Shrew.

Lost, friendless, with shriveling hopes and dwindling supplies, the shrew pedaled the houseboat away from the spider island and toward nowhere in particular.

Chapter 19

The moon cast slithering shadows inside the houseboat. The previous day's adventure had left Archie exhausted and dehydrated. He woke up terribly thirsty. With eyesight too poor to see properly in the dim light, the shrew climbed down from his bunk and began to feel and scent his way toward the small container of fresh water they kept inside.

But something smelled wrong. He recognized the warm, furry odor of Mr. Popli, the hunger-inducing aroma of their new barnacle stash, and the ever-present smells of the open sea. He detected something else, too—something animal. His fur bristled, and he reached back into his bunk for Mr. Popli's knife. Had they crashed into another island in the night? Had the spiders found them? Were new enemies surrounding the *Abigail*?

The shrew inhaled deeply through his snout and

bared his teeth. He knew the scent but couldn't place it. And then he realized. It smelled like . . . Colubra!

Few things unsettle an inventor more than being presented with contradicting facts. His nose told him Colubra was nearby. His brain told him there was absolutely no way Colubra could be close. They'd traveled too far in the wrong direction and had not had nearly enough time to make it back. Unless . . .

What if a rip current has been moving our island at the same rate we've been traveling? What if Colubra has been looking for us this whole time, furious about the egg? What if the egg—Something rubbery squished under Archie's foot. He reached down and picked it up.

The object in his hand felt thin and leathery, broken, yet still slightly round. He held it up to the light and squinted. *The egg! It's hatched! Oh, thank goodness.*

He lifted it to his nose. He'd expected an avian smell, some sort of bird like Merri. But whatever had just hatched from inside *this particular* egg smelled exactly like . . . like . . . a snake.

The fur on Archie's ears tingled as a hissing sound emanated from across the boat. "I am starving," came a low, reptilian voice. "Mother, is there something to eat?"

And then he realized exactly what had happened. *Oh, snakespit.*

Archie stood frozen.

I rescued an egg from Colubra. No. I stole a snake egg from Colubra. No. I kidnapped Colubra's child. And now we have a hungry snake. Inside the boat. In the dark of night. If this baby snake does not eat me, Mr. Popli will throw me overboard. And Colubra, if she ever finds us, will be even less forgiving. But first things first. There is a hungry snake inside the boat.

As quietly and gently as possible, Archie woke Mr. Popli and helped him up to the top deck of the *Abigail*, whispering the whole way that he would explain everything in a moment. With the effects of the spider poison lingering in his bloodstream, Mr. Popli had fallen in and out of consciousness all day and into the night. Right now, he was mostly lucid.

"What's going on, Archibald? I'm hardly well enough to be moving around like this," Mr. Popli said as he leaned back against the steering mechanism.

"The egg hatched."

"That's good news, I suppose. But why are we on the roof?"

"The baby; it's not a bird."

"Really? What is it then? Surely the egg was too big for it to be an insect. A lizard? A toad? It's not a toad, I hope. We'll have a devil of a time feeding it."

"It's not a toad."

"Well, then, what on earth is it?"

"It's long . . ."

"A stick bug?"

"And a reptile . . ."

"A gecko?"

"With scales . . ."

"An iguana? Really, Archibald. I've no patience for games. What is it?"

"It might answer to Little Colubra."

Archie winced as he said it. He waited for Mr. Popli to lash out. To scream at him for causing another disaster. For endangering yet again everyone and everything they knew and cared about.

But all Mr. Popli could manage was "Oh."

"I think it's a boy," the shrew added hopefully. "And it believes I'm its mother."

"Oh, my. Well, then I suppose you'd better go down there and kill it." Then Mr. Popli curled into a ball and fell back asleep.

《 》

Kill it? Archie thought, climbing back down through the hatch. *But it's just a baby. What if it turns out to be a nice sort of snake? What if it's a vegetarian?* He would have sooner cannonballed into a school of feeding mackerel than hurt another living creature needlessly.

"Helloooo-ooooh," he whispered, sniffing the air and feeling for vibrations along the plastic walls of the houseboat. "Little baby snaaa-aaaaake. I'm your mommmmmy."

The shrew's eyes shifted rapidly around the room. He'd waited till the sun was rising to go back inside the *Abigail*. "If I'm going to get eaten, I'd at least like to see what's gnawing on me," he'd told the fevered Mr. Popli. Although now he wasn't so sure.

He could still smell the snake in the room, but the scent had spread. It seemed this snake had explored the whole interior of the houseboat. *Probably just trying to find a nice mushroom or some leafy greens for breakfast.* Using the ropes that crisscrossed the interior, Archie scrabbled from stem to stern through the open air but caught no glimpse of the snake. His fur bristled at every shadow, expecting a hiss, a glimmer of fangs, and a slow, painful ride down a dark throat.

Finally, and with a long sigh, he dropped to the bottom of the hull and began tiptoeing toward the front of the *Abigail*, poking at every nook and cranny with Mr. Popli's long knife. *What does one say to a ravenous, shrew-eating snake that one has accidentally kidnapped? "Oh hello there, Mr. Snake. Would you like to try some* of these delicious salted barnacles? They're the only thing we have to eat." Somehow he imagined the snake would be happy to expand the menu.

The scent grew stronger as he approached the bunks. Everything he saw turned serpentine in his mind. That pile of sheets. This bit of rope. The tool belt hanging from his nightstand.

And then he saw it. Or thought he did. A wiggle, a shirk, a whisper of movement. From inside his bed. Underneath his very own blanket. *And now we see what you're made of, Archie Shrew.* He might have stabbed the knife straight through the blanket. He could have swept up the tangle of sheets and thrown the whole thing into the ocean. But instead, Archie Shrew did something brave and not very smart. Using the tip of Mr. Popli's knife, he peeled back the covers and gasped.

It was the smallest snake he'd ever seen, not even as big around as his tail. Certainly not big enough to eat a shrew (or a mouse). And it was fast asleep.

"I think I'll call you Huxley."

Chapter 20

Hundreds of eyes followed the shrew's descent into the depths. They neither attacked nor fled. *Don't make eye contact*, Archie told himself. *Pretend like you don't even see them and they'll ignore you.* Archie held the pole tightly in his paw, Mr. Popli's glass knife lashed to one end. A stretch of rubber band created tension against the fur on his forearm.

Once Archie sank beneath the school of menhaden, he paused and counted to five in his head. Suspended and perfectly still below the surface, he admired the deep blue extending beneath him as far as he could see. Large, blurry fish shadows patrolled the edges of his field of vision, but they were so far away it seemed he could pinch them between two fingers. Still, they watched the shrew with curiosity.

He picked out a target and kicked once toward the surface. Aiming the spear as he turned, he let go as soon as the fish was in its path. The spear, propelled

163

by the rubber band, shot out of his paw like an arrow to hit the menhaden. The rest of the school scattered.

The unlucky fish, roughly half the size of the shrew, was impaled halfway up the spear and dove downward. Archie, beginning to lose his breath, fumbled with the rope that connected the spear to his arm. The larger predators below took notice of the struggling menhaden and began to ascend.

Archie kicked toward sunlight, locked in a deadly game of tug-of-war. With every flick of the fish's tail, Archie was yanked farther down. With every upward kick, he lost a little more breath. Meanwhile, the predators circled closer. Another second and he'd have to let go of the line. But the shrew broke the surface just in time, transferring the rope to Mr. Popli's outstretched paw.

Archie scrambled out of the water. Still weak from the spider bite, Mr. Popli could not fight the fish for long. The rope slipped in his paw. A shadow beneath the surface raced toward the boat. Archie slid down next to Mr. Popli and grabbed hold of the rope, hauling the menhaden paw over paw up the water barrel. As he pulled it onto the top, an enormous striped wahoo exploded out of the water, barely missing Archie's outstretched paw. The wahoo arced alongside the *Abigail*, then splashed down a tail's length in front of them.

Archie grinned, holding his flopping catch as he caught his breath.

"One way or another," Mr. Popli told the gasping shrew. "Your pet snake is going to be the death of us both."

Inside the *Abigail*, Huxley slithered hungrily toward the smell of fresh fish.

They'd tried to make him a vegetarian, offering algae and nori they'd collected, chopped up, and seasoned with sea salt. But the infant reptile had refused everything, even the brown, leathery meat of the gooseneck barnacles Mr. Popli had harvested from the spiders' island. Without food, the snake had become more and more lethargic. So Archie had decided to go fishing.

Mr. Popli hated himself for it, but he secretly hoped the snake would not survive its infancy. *It would be much easier that way*, the mouse reasoned. *No one knows about it but the two of us, not even Colubra. We'd never have to tell another soul.*

But a bond had grown between the snake and the shrew. Archie lulled Huxley to sleep on his chest, the rhythmic roll of the waves syncopating with the steady beat of his heart.

It had been Archie's idea to create the spear and shoot it underwater with the rubber band. He'd begged

Mr. Popli to borrow his knife for the experiment. It was only after hours of badgering that the mouse consented.

"But if you lose my knife, I'll make a new one of your shinbone." The shrew had little doubt that Mr. Popli meant it.

Now, watching Huxley unhinge his jaw to swallow the big chunks of fish Archie tossed to him, Mr. Popli wished he hadn't enabled Archie's invention. "No good will come of this," he warned. "This creature has a taste for meat, and I wouldn't be surprised if we both end up in its gullet. I can only hope it eats you first."

"It likes me," Archie replied, patting the snake on the head. "So you'd probably save me for last, wouldn't you, Huxley?"

The snake nodded vigorously, then gulped down another chunk of menhaden.

"Stop calling it that! You're going to get attached. And when it grows into a full-sized carnivore, you'll be sorely disappointed. You'll also be dinner."

The tiny snake was no threat to them now, but it was growing by the day. "It's a living thing," said the shrew. "And it's a baby. We can raise it to only eat fish. Maybe you can even train it to protect the island."

"Snakes are killers," said Mr. Popli. "They can't be reasoned with."

The mention of the island only deepened Mr. Popli's

concern. What would Colubra do if they came back with her kidnapped son? Even now, there could be a war raging if she merely suspected the islanders were involved in the loss of her egg. No, the snake could never be allowed to return with them to the island, regardless of Archibald's attachment.

Archie, too, worried about their return. Here he was, on the precise adventure he'd been hoping for, in a machine of his own design, with every opportunity to search for the family he missed so much. And he looked for them. At the crest of every wave, in the shadow of every cloud, he sought signs of life. But the ocean persisted in relentless emptiness. A suspicion began to take root that perhaps the family he dreamed of was only a memory. And perhaps he'd turned his back on the only family he had left.

The *Abigail* continued on a southeast heading, although Archie was unsure if this was the right direction. *At least we're getting farther from those spiders*, thought the shrew. *It's nice to not worry about being eaten for a change.*

« »

The shrew awoke to a flash of fangs and the flicker of a forked tongue against his eyelids. The snake wrapped Archie in his coils and squeezed.

"Good morning, Huxley!" said the shrew, yawning.

"My instinct is to eat you."

"Indeed!"

"I'll soon be sufficiently sized."

"Yes, yes."

"I suspect that you would taste similar to fish."

"I certainly hope not! I'd like to think that I would taste a bit sweeter. And crunchier."

Archie and Huxley gently leaned their heads together as they laughed. The snake was growing quickly with his steady diet of menhaden. He'd even shed his skin.

It had been three weeks since Huxley hatched, and the sea snake could now fish on his own and for the crew. Soon he would be too heavy to perch on Archie's shoulder. Already the shrew buckled under Huxley's girth. And although they now had plenty of food and summer rains provided fresh water, both Mr. Popli and Archie worried that they might never again find the island.

"We should turn a bit more south today," said Huxley. His tone was matter-of-fact, as though it were an indisputable truth. "We're close to home."

"Wait! How can you know that?! Some sort of homing instinct?" asked Archie.

Even Mr. Popli's ears perked up at the comment. The snake nodded. "It says we're getting close."

By day's end, they'd begun to pass familiar areas, including a sargassum patch littered with hundreds of bobbing rubber duckies.

"It's the fabled ducky patch!" announced Archie. "I've always wondered if it was real. Can we get one?"

"Why?" questioned Mr. Popli. "They float past the island all the time."

"The *Abigail* could use a masthead. And besides, duckies are lucky!"

"We've been gone for over a month, hopelessly lost, facing daily, deadly perils. Now we're finally within sniffing distance of home and you want us to stop so you can wrestle a rubber duck on board and then attach it to my beloved houseboat?!"

"Yes!"

"Absolutely not!"

Archie's ears drooped. "Please?"

"No."

"Please?"

"Will it make you stop asking?"

"Yes."

"Fine. But make it quick," the mouse huffed. "Duckies are lucky, indeed. What nonsense!"

Chapter 21

Huxley's instinct may have sensed their proximity to home, but it could not anticipate the shark. The long, crooked dorsal fin divided the surface of the water, swaying back and forth indifferently—almost as if it had nowhere in particular to go and all the time in the world to get there.

The *Abigail* veered right. So did the fin. They tracked to the left. The fin followed.

"It's been tailing us for ten minutes. Tiger shark, I should think." Mr. Popli handed the looking glass to Archie. "This is bad."

"Very," the shrew replied.

"Do you have any brilliant ideas?"

"We're riding the ocean in a flimsy plastic bottle pursued by a species known to eat everything from old tires to fur coats. No, I don't have any ideas. Unless you'd like to salt and pepper yourself. I'm confident we would make excellent appetizers."

"Archibald!"

"What? Do you think of yourself as more of a dessert?"

"Could you be serious for one minute?!"

"Sorry!" Archie pulled the brake lever to bring the houseboat to a stop.

"What are you doing?!"

"We can't outrun it. We may as well let it know that we know it's here."

"That's quite possibly the worst idea you've ever had."

But no sooner did the *Abigail* turn toward the shark than the fin descended.

"It's stalking us," said Huxley. "It doesn't like to be observed."

"Wonderful," said Mr. Popli. "Now we can wait for it to attack us from underneath."

"Yes," Huxley agreed. "Let's not sit still."

Archie shrugged, releasing the brake lever to allow the paddle wheel to churn once more. Slowly the *Abigail* chugged forward. Within a minute, the fin surfaced behind them, only closer this time. And now with every swish of its powerful tail, the tiger shark was closing the distance.

They tried to think of ways to rid themselves of their persistent pursuer.

"Killer whales eat sharks," said Archie. "Can anyone make noises like an orca?" They tried making whale sounds. The shark was not impressed.

"Is your new arrow launcher finished? Can you shoot it in the eye?" asked Mr. Popli.

"Yes. And a great idea! If you jump overboard and start swimming around, I'll have a perfect shot right as it comes up to swallow you."

"Well, then I don't know what else to do!" said Mr. Popli. "Stuff its gills?"

"Bite it on the nose?" suggested Huxley.

None of their ideas, it seemed, would give them a fighting chance.

"We're no match for a tiger shark," said the mouse.

"A match!" said Archie. "That's just the thing! But we've got to act quickly. We'll need the supplies from the spider island."

"And then?"

"All we'll have to do is get the shark to attack us."

《 》

Once Archie had explained it, Mr. Popli was no longer convinced it was the worst idea the shrew had ever had. Perhaps only the second or third worst. But, having no better plan, they went ahead with it.

Using his glass knife, Mr. Popli scraped the sandpaper-like stuff from the side of the matchbox into a pile. He poured it onto a wedge of aluminum foil next to the shrew.

"Careful!" said Archie. "It's highly combustible when it all mixes together."

"Explain it one more time," said the mouse.

"When the stuff from the side of the matchbox rubs up against the stuff from the tips of the matches, it makes a tiny explosion."

"And the bigger we make this pile of stuff—"

"—the bigger the blast!" Archie finished his sentence.

"How many matches?" asked Huxley, carrying three more between his jaws.

"All of them."

They rushed through the work, leaving the houseboat momentarily without a pilot. They could easily replot their course as long as they didn't have to do so from the belly of the shark.

When they'd finished, Mr. Popli lifted the wedge of aluminum foil, piled with all of the explosive powder that they'd harvested from the waterproof matches. "So what do we do with all of this?" he asked.

"We stuff it inside an old friend," said the shrew. "Then we go fishing!"

Chapter 22

Archie slit the rubber ducky along its back, then held open the cut while Mr. Popli stuffed the cavity with crumples of aluminum foil.

"Hurry," hissed Huxley.

"This is not necessarily the type of thing one should rush!" Archie whispered as Mr. Popli carefully placed the explosive packet into the cradle made by the aluminum foil. Archie anxiously released his hold on the gash, allowing the thick rubber to close almost as if it had never been cut open at all.

"Now how are we going to get it into the water?" asked Mr. Popli.

"Delicately."

Suddenly the houseboat lurched and the duck tumbled off the deck and into the ocean. A massive head rolled out of the water. Rows of jagged teeth marched past the trio, followed by a speckled eye with an almond-shaped pupil.

"It's now or never!" yelled the mouse.

"Is it too late to pick never?" Archie whined.

In response, Mr. Popli leapt to the helm and yanked the brake release, pushing them to full speed. A rope made from every shred of string they could salvage stretched between them and the ducky. When the line ran out, the ducky surged to life, skiing two shark lengths behind the *Abigail*.

The tiger shark turned in pronounced patterns, arching its back and flaring its tail as it circled the houseboat. They could easily make out the rippled stripes down its side and tail. It paused to consider their bait, breaching halfheartedly and bumping the rubber ducky with its nose. They held their breath.

"Just a nibble!" begged Archie. "A tiny taste!" But the shark submerged and circled slowly around. It surfaced again, this time knocking the ducky with its dorsal fin. Then it turned toward the *Abigail*. The trap had failed.

Archie fired arrows at the shark from his new launcher. They bounced harmlessly off its broad back. When he ran out of arrows, he flung bottle caps.

"It's no good, Archibald," said Mr. Popli. "It wants a meal. And we're it. I suppose we all have to get ready to jump and see if maybe one or two of us can get away."

They were out of weapons. Out of tricks. Out of luck.

And then it was Huxley's turn to have a terrible idea. He slithered up to Archie and, without warning, struck at the shrew.

Defensively, Archie swept his arrow launcher toward the snake. The pointed tip cut across the snake's belly, leaving a thin red line.

"Why did you do that?" Archie demanded. "I could have killed you!"

"The shark needs to be enticed," said Huxley. And without another word he slithered off the side of the boat and into the ocean.

"Huxley! Wait!" Archie yelled. He tried to jump in after the juvenile snake but Mr. Popli tackled him to the deck.

The shrew fought to free himself from the mouse's grip, but Mr. Popli held firm. *We had to get rid of it sometime. And at least this way the snake made its own decision. Not that Archibald will ever forgive me for stopping him.*

Huxley swam right over the shadow of the shark toward the trap they'd set. He wrapped himself around the rubber ducky and squeezed. A big ruby red drop of blood rolled down the side of the duck and into the ocean.

As if an alarm had gone off in the shark's head, it spun excitedly toward the trap, now baited by Huxley. The fin submerged.

Huxley looked at Archie and flicked his tongue, as near to a smile as a snake could manage.

Archie—still gripped tightly by Mr. Popli—yelled and motioned wildly for him to swim back.

The snake looked both ways as if he were going to cross a path. He began to slide off the ducky, back toward the houseboat.

Archie relaxed. It was going to be all right. Mr. Popli helped him up.

The shark launched out of the water, upper jaw extending to reveal layers of jagged, mismatched teeth. Rubber ducky and snake sailed skyward in its mouth. Huxley twisted sideways, landing on the shark's snout.

The jaws snapped. The explosive cracked.

A tooth ricocheted into the side of the houseboat.

Everything splashed down together.

The *Abigail*, still tied to the ducky, surged toward the shark. The predator surfaced, thrashing its head wildly at the burning sensation and the taste of sulfur. Smoke poured from its open mouth.

The houseboat jolted and jerked. "Cut the line!" Mr. Popli shouted, clinging to the steering mechanism.

The shark rolled on the surface, wrapping the line

around itself and pulling the *Abigail* toward a whirlpool of flailing fins and slashing teeth.

Archie reached for the rope with both paws and began to bite.

It surprised him how quickly the line snapped free and the houseboat rocked backward from the shark. Archie grabbed hold of the trailing end of the rope to keep from being thrown into the sea. Exhilaration raced through his veins. He'd never felt so *animal* before.

Mr. Popli pedaled away as quickly as he could.

"Wait! Where's Huxley?"

The mouse pulled back on the brake for a moment, considering. The snake had just saved their lives. *But it's a snake.* It hadn't chosen to be born a snake any more than he'd chosen to be born a mouse. *But it's Colubra's son.* It was a life. And it was in danger. *But Colubra destroyed my home!* Everything he'd built, everything he believed in, depended on the possibility that natural enemies could live in harmony if they chose to do so.

Mr. Popli made his choice.

"Okay," he said. "Let's go find Huxley."

《 》

Sunlight glinted off black and white scales bobbing on the ocean's surface. Mr. Popli saw Huxley first and dove in from the top deck.

179

He wrapped the snake around his torso as he began treading water. Huxley gave a tiny squeeze before laying his head on the mouse's shoulder. With that small gesture, a wash of fatherly instinct overcame Mr. Popli. Suddenly he understood both Archie and Huxley in a different way.

"Everything's going to be all right," he told the snake.

"I bit it on the nose," the snake whispered.

"What?"

"The shark. I said we should bite it on the nose. I did. Did it work?"

"Yes, Huxley. It worked."

Archie helped Mr. Popli carry the listless snake on board.

"How is he?" asked the shrew.

"He'll live," Mr. Popli replied. And he realized he was happy about it.

Chapter 23

"Pie," said Archie. "Mushroom pie. Seaweed pie. Squid-kidney pie. Pie of every kind. Pie of any kind! I don't care as long as it's pie."

"For me it's Old Lady Toad's dandelion tea," Mr. Popli replied. "With fresh barnacle bread right out of the oven." The mouse huffed and puffed as he pedaled the *Abigail*, guided by Huxley's internal compass, toward the growing speck on the horizon.

Home. Mr. Popli wondered whether the citizens had been able to repair the wall. He worried what conflicts Edward the Dung had stirred up. He hoped beyond hope to see the flutter of a small yellow bird.

Archie turned to smile at the juvenile snake. "I don't suppose you *could* miss anything about home, could you, Huxley?" asked Archie. "You were just an egg."

"There was darkness," said the snake. "And warmness. And . . . music."

"Music?" Mr. Popli thought about the former mouse colony and all that had been there before Colubra's arrival. He remembered many sounds, but nothing at all like music.

"No, not music," the snake mused. "A song."

"Colubra—I mean, your mother. She sang to you?!" asked Mr. Popli, intrigued.

"Yes!" said Huxley, recalling. "A slow, wishful song. About bright scales and soft nests and hatchlings, safe and warm."

"Oh." Mr. Popli had only ever considered Colubra as an enemy and a predator, never as a mother. Especially not the kind who would sing lullabies to her unhatched eggs.

Familiar flotsam now littered the waterway. The iceberg-like corner of a pine casket. The gilded masthead of an ancient dragon boat. Mr. Popli exhaled a deep sigh.

"What is it?" asked Archie.

"It's just . . . We're nearly home. It's been too long since we've seen friendly waters."

With a whistle and a splash, a projectile sailed right over their heads and into the sea three waves away. The friends looked anxiously to see what had nearly hit them.

"TURN BACK OR PREPARE TO SINK!" a voice thundered. "THESE WATERS ARE CLOSED!"

A sailboat the size of a washtub (in fact, it had once been a washtub) came round from behind a bobbing whiskey barrel. Armed lizards and armored beetles lined the forecastle and main decks.

"Ahoy!" yelled Mr. Popli, waving his arms. "It's Mayor Popli and Archibald Shrew! Ahoy!"

Captain Shift, the same gecko who had served as bailiff during Archie's trial, stared down at them from the much larger boat. Mr. Popli noticed that neither she nor her companions wore the symbol of the Order of the Silver Moon any longer.

"It certainly sounds like you, Mayor Popli," said Captain Shift. "But these are strange times. And I'm under orders that anyone approaching the island should be turned back."

"I assure you, we are friends!" said the mouse. "And citizens! We must be allowed to come home. Who gave these orders? Who's in charge now?"

The gecko paused. She looked careworn as she glanced back and forth to the hardened faces on either side of her. Mr. Popli could tell that she wanted to believe him, to help. Something was wrong and she wished the mouse could make it right. All he had to do was convince her that he was on her side.

Only then did she notice Huxley, hiding between Archie's legs. "SNAKE!" the gecko yelled. At once all of the soldiers lifted heavy spears with sharp, metallic blades that looked easily capable of piercing the houseboat's insubstantial hull, not to mention small, castaway animals.

"I can explain," said Mr. Popli.

"No more talking. This is the last warning you get. If I see this boat again, I will sink it." A look of warning in the gecko's eye assured Mr. Popli that she meant it.

The mouse pedaled the *Abigail* away from the patrol ship.

"Well," he said, "that was not quite the welcome I was hoping for."

"I was just hoping for pie," Archie huffed.

"Something's wrong. We need to get home to figure out what it is."

"But they've threatened to sink our ship!"

"Let them try."

《 》

The catapult payloads resembled oversized sand burrs made of glass and jagged metal, held together with muck and string. Another one slammed into the side of the *Abigail*. Dauntless, she chugged onward toward the

186

island—although slowed down by the armor they'd scabbed to her hull. Hard-shell plastic packaging, disposable coffee lids, and can cozies covered her sides like scales.

But the night watch guards were expert shots. One by one, projectiles dislodged armor and pierced her plastic sides. With each direct hit she crumpled a bit more and slipped a little lower into the water. Eventually, the engine no longer had the thrust to propel her forward. Only the tip of the coil spring could be seen above the waterline. The *Abigail* had sunk.

Chapter 24

When Archie had revealed the existence of the secret entrance under the Watchtower, he'd thought the mouse would be livid. They'd just finished attaching the armor to the houseboat.

"There's something I've been meaning to tell you. There *might* be another way into the island."

"There might?"

"Well, technically speaking, by *might* I mean there *is*."

But Mr. Popli had beamed at the news, calling the shrew a "clever little genius." And so, instead of chugging full speed toward the wall inside the *Abigail*, they'd wound the spring as tight as it would go and set her on a collision course with the gate.

《 》

As the sun came up, Archie, Mr. Popli, and Huxley swam behind a rubber duck, pushing it in front of them under the looming Watchtower, hoping to disguise their presence. As it happened, they didn't need the duck. All guards had been sent to the front gate to defend the island from the *Abigail*. The trio safely slunk through the secret door.

"I hate all this scurrying and hiding! I'm the mayor! I'll go straight to the council!" Mr. Popli exploded as soon as Archie had carefully closed the door behind them.

"No. You're an enemy intruder who was threatened with death should you do exactly what we're doing right now."

"I don't like it one bit. It makes me feel like a criminal!"

"You get used to it."

Mr. Popli thoughtfully considered Archie's comment. *Is this how Archie always feels? No one trusts him because he doesn't follow the rules. And he doesn't follow the rules because no one trusts him. No wonder he's always in trouble.*

Not daring to use the main thoroughfares, the trio clambered over a laundry detergent bottle and into the recess of a length of Styrofoam packing. Archie helped Huxley up, over, and down. From there, they watched passersby on a section of the driftwood highway that connected parts of the island.

"Something's definitely wrong," said the mouse

eventually. "Everyone has their heads down. No one's laughing. No one's talking. We'd better stay out of sight until we can figure out what's what. Archibald, your workshop would be the perfect place to hide out!"

"A brilliant idea! If it wasn't boarded up and locked tight, remember? Even I couldn't break in. And I may have possibly tried."

"Oh, no. And Merri had the key. Wait—you did *what*?"

"Only six or seven times. But let's focus on what's important here. If you gave the key to Merri, where would she keep it?"

"In her perch."

They looked inland. From the center of the island Merri's perch ascended—an impenetrable fortress atop an impossible climb of jagged metal. Built from scraps no one else wanted, in a place no other islander would consider, Merri had created a home that did not exactly invite casual guests. In fact, neither shrew nor mouse had ever been up to visit.

Archie's whiskers shuddered. "Shall we play odds and evens to see who goes climbing?"

"I'll take evens."

"Ready? One, two, three."

"Snakespit," said Mr. Popli.

Chapter 25

Fierce wind buffeted Mr. Popli. His tail flapped behind him. A paw lost its grip. He looked down and immediately wished he hadn't. *A rope might have been a good idea. Especially on the way down.*

Carefully, but with many a nick and scratch, the mouse negotiated his way toward the nest towering high above the island. From the outside, Merri's home looked as inviting as a serpent's den—it was supported by a broken metal pipe pockmarked with serrated holes and flaking rust. At the pinnacle sat an orb of tangled wires, interwoven with sharp slivers of hardened plastic. The only entrance was a tiny hole, promising danger to any trespasser. It resembled ammunition for the catapult more than a home.

Hanging below the nest, Mr. Popli marveled at its construction. The sphere was perfect in shape and balance—no mouse could have done better. Without a single tool or anyone's help, Merri had built the most

impenetrable structure on the island. Shards of colored glass spiked out from the equally dangerous woven mesh at irregular intervals, making it as beautiful as it was daunting.

Using the tiny claws at the tips of his fingers, Mr. Popli found paw-holds between the plastic, glass, and metal. He gripped with one paw. Then the other. Slow as the rising moon, he picked his way under and across Merri's nest. It was like climbing through a jungle of twisted fangs. The wind, still gusting, drove his body against a tangled fray of wire. He winced and let go with one paw. *At least we didn't try Archibald's idea of launching me up here in a catapult.*

He regained his grip, stretched as far as his legs would allow, and grabbed ahold of a dangling spike that jutted from the entrance. With a heave and a long scratch down his belly, Mr. Popli pulled himself into Merri's nest.

He paused just inside the entrance. Shattered light sent shadows dancing across the interior. Mr. Popli had expected the home of a warrior, sparse and spartan. What he found made his heart clog his throat.

For all of its intimidating exterior, the inside of Merri's home resembled a museum. Photographs and drawings filled the space, covering the floors, walls, and ceiling. And all were images of birds! Mr. Popli recognized herons and eagles and wrens. There were dozens of other birds he'd never seen or heard of. What Merri hadn't salvaged from the garbage, she'd drawn with her beak or crudely outlined with lengths of string. This was the work of an artist.

Mr. Popli stepped farther in. A shadow twitched above his head. He spun, drawing his knife. It was the shape and size of a bird. "Merri?" He squinted and saw not one but a dozen shapes perched high in the shadows! They all looked ready to swoop down on the mouse.

Mr. Popli had fought outnumbered more times than he could count, but a single bird could outmaneuver and overpower a mouse with ease. Where had they come from? How had they gotten onto the island unnoticed? His muscles tensed, he bared his teeth and prepared for an attack. But it never came.

And then a ray of light shined through one of the birds. They were hollow—sculptures assembled from bits of trash woven together with fine thread. Glass beads and gleaming buttons looked like real eyes. They balanced impossibly and beautifully, filling the room with an impression of life. He relaxed and put his knife back in the sheath tied to his leg.

Deeper inside, Mr. Popli saw the key. It hung on a hook next to a sweeping mural that covered a large section of the east wall. As he got closer, he recognized it as a map of the island. He gaped at the detailed depiction, along with Colubra's lair to the north and other smaller patches of garbage beyond the wall. And then he saw the lines. Merri had drawn dotted lines radiating out from their island, some longer, some shorter. There were hundreds.

This must be every place she's flown! And look at the different animals! Mr. Popli noted drawings of insects and reptiles and mammals in their colonies, well outside the range of their ships. But this map was so much more detailed than the crude ones he'd seen other animals make. Merri had trimmed her drawing with ornate flourishes. She used elegant patterns to contrast islands and the sea. It was as beautiful, in its own way, as her statues.

The mouse hung the key around his neck, his paw lingering to trace the map. Garbage Island only wanted Merri the messenger. Merri the worker. Merri the warrior. He saw that. *But still, Merri, why did you keep your creativity hidden away?*

Without warning, a feathery shadow zipped past him into the room. It was like the twitching shadows of the false birds above him, but this one was real. Mr. Popli felt the rush of wind. Startled, he backpedaled toward the entrance. The shadowy figure spun. Mr. Popli took another step backward. He was teetering on the edge of the entryway. A whisker farther and he'd fall.

"Mr. Popli?" came a voice.

His foot slipped. And then Mr. Popli fell.

Chapter 26

A dozen thoughts raced through Mr. Popli's mind. Visions of his mother. Colubra. The war. Even Archibald.

A claw seized his tail. Mr. Popli swung into the side of Merri's nest, his head racing toward a needlelike splinter of glass. He spun his head sideways and bit down on the glass. It cracked. So did a tooth.

"Mayor Popli? It can't be!"

"Yes," the mouse answered, dangling. "And I could use a bit of assistance."

Merri held his tail till Mr. Popli found grips for his claws. Slowly, he climbed back into her nest.

Once inside, she hopped and fluttered excitedly, peppering the mouse with feathery hugs and kisses.

"It's good to see you, too," he said, surprised. In all his time, he'd never seen Merri express this kind of affection, except maybe with Archibald.

"What about Archie?" asked the bird.

"Alive and impetuous as ever. But you'll never guess what happened!"

"You stole an egg from Colubra and out hatched a baby snake?"

Mr. Popli's eyebrows bristled in surprise. "But—how would you know?"

"Since we lost you, Colubra's been attacking the island every day. Different times. Different tactics. Raving about her kidnapped egg. Somehow, one of her snake skins washed up against the wall and got stuck on it. She thinks the islanders did it to taunt her. An envoy was sent, members of the Order. Angus, Mildred, and Lester. They never came back. She won't stop until she figures out how to tear down the wall. I don't even think she wants to eat the citizens. She just wants the island . . . exterminated."

Mayor Popli sat down hard. It was worse than he'd imagined. Could they escape? Abandon the island and flee as the mice had when she'd come to the colony? But then Mr. Popli thought of old Mrs. Toad. She wouldn't last a week on the open sea. He thought of the dozens of members of the Order who had volunteered, at his request, to risk life and limb for this dream. Colubra was a riddle he had to solve.

"The whole island is in a panic. There's a war council with representatives from each of the clans.

Edward the Dung is in charge, and he's handled things like a real dung beetle. No one knows what to do."

"What's happened to the Order?"

"All conscripted into military service. The lifesaving boats converted to warships. The volunteers turned into soldiers." The thought made Mr. Popli's stomach turn. The Order of the Silver Moon had been established as a rescue squad, trained to save lives. Not to fight.

"Oh Merri! But how did you make it back? Why didn't you sound the bell?"

Then Merri told him how she'd raced the storm to the island and lost, getting dashed by the driving wind into a wave. How a hurt wing had kept her from taking off again. How she'd flapped and fluttered to the wall as lightning crashed and the waves grew. How no one had heard her call for help. How she'd spent the night clinging to a drifting scrap of Styrofoam.

"They found me the next day, but wouldn't let me fly to look for you. I'm afraid I pecked poor Nurse Salamander right on the shin when she refused to take the splint off my wing. And then Colubra came and it's been a crisis every day since. But you're home! Let's go get Archie and meet with the council. With the two of you back, a plan can be made to set things right. I just know it."

Chapter 27

They're going to murder us. I just know it. Archie peered through the tiny metal mesh of the cage in which he and Huxley were trapped. Dozens of angry citizens surrounded them.

What had happened was this: Archie, having become bored while waiting on Mr. Popli, had a wonderful (terrible) idea.

"Would you like to see the city, Huxley?"

"Is it wise? It seems we should stay in one place."

"Don't worry. I grew up in this heap. I know every nook and cranny. Wait till you see the algae beds being harvested across the lagoon! Smell the fish pies from the bakers' square!"

The notion of fish pies was too good for Huxley to pass up. When the soldiers caught them, reclining in an alleyway, each licking bits of pilfered fish pie from their faces, they knew they were in deep trouble.

"Snakespit," said Huxley.

Merri and Mr. Popli arrived just in time. Few of the citizens had ever seen Colubra, and many assumed that they'd caught her sneaking into the island, that she was now caged with Archie.

"She doesn't look so big!"

"Hand me that spear, I'll solve all our problems right now!"

"Try it and you'll learn to fly the hard way." Merri landed in a fury, every feather puffed to make her look twice her size. A wild gleam pulsed in her eyes. Mr. Popli had never seen her so menacing, so fierce. *This* was the bird the citizens feared.

The offending party stumbled backward, pushing the crowd away from the cage.

"Merri?" asked Archie, pressing his face up against the mesh.

"Hello, Archie. You're in a squall of trouble."

« »

News spread quickly of a snake on the island, rumors of Colubra being captured alongside a traitorous accomplice. The war council gathered for an emergency session, and Mr. Popli found himself seated, with Archie, in a familiar plastic cereal bowl. No one, not even Merri, would consider letting Huxley out of the cage beside them.

Edward the Dung ambled to the mayor's seat—the one that Mr. Popli used to occupy. He sat down, looking smug as a bug.

"We're doomed, aren't we?" asked the shrew.

"I should think so."

"Captain Shift," said the dung beetle. "Can you tell us what you witnessed last night?"

The gecko cleared her throat. "Honorable war council members, I led the patrol last night on the southern approach. At dusk, we witnessed a vessel making its way toward the island. Per the war council's orders, we fired a warning shot and commanded her to turn back. They hailed us. We allowed them to advance. The mouse announced himself as Mayor Popli and invoked his right as a citizen to access the island. I considered escorting them in myself until we saw the snake."

Someone in the audience gasped at the mention of the snake, as though Huxley wasn't sitting right there in the assembly hall, smelling the unfamiliar air with a flickering tongue. Mr. Popli rolled his eyes and put a paw to his shaking head. Captain Shift continued.

"I followed protocol. No outsiders were to be allowed in on threat of death, so we turned them back. That was the last we saw of them."

"Thank you for your testimony, Captain." The

beetle turned toward Mr. Popli, Archie, and Huxley. All eyes followed his gaze. "It's a shame you didn't bury them at sea and save us the trouble."

Edward the Dung believed himself to be the best leader, which is often the worst kind of person for the job. He grew up a bully, and not even a very good one. Most animals mistook his attempts to torment others as a mild developmental impediment.

He'd run against Mayor Popli in the last two elections and had lost, both times, in landslides. And yet, with Mr. Popli gone and no small amount of voter fraud, he was now chair of the war council. And he was enjoying it immensely. From this position he could, on threat of death, demand the admiration he'd always wanted but never earned. Not only that, but others did his dirty work. It was little wonder the island was in a state of panic.

He addressed the pair of bedraggled mammals. "You've been accused of harboring an enemy and defying orders by sneaking into the island!" If a dung beetle could appear villainously elated, Edward the Dung certainly did. "Please, explain yourselves to this war council. Then we will proceed to the hanging." The rest of the citizens tensed. No one clicked a pincer or licked an eyeball.

"What a blowhard," whispered Mr. Popli to Archie.

"Yes," the shrew agreed solemnly. "He's got all the qualities of a fine leader."

"Shall I go ahead and put him in his place?"

"With Godspeed, Mr. Mayor."

"WHAT ARE YOU TWO WHISPERING ABOUT?!" The dung beetle's head turned from shiny green to a dull orange, which is as close as it could get to red.

Mr. Popli cleared his voice and rose up to his full height. "As mayor, I hereby disband the war council. Thank you, Mr. Dung, for your service. You may step down."

"But—"

"No. No. You've done more than enough harm. Our citizens are in a panic. An enemy threatens our borders. And you appear to have handled the situation like a frogfish."

"You can't disband the war council!" The beetle stomped his six feet and clacked his mandibles in absolute outrage. "You're being tried for treason!"

"Tried, perhaps. But never formally arrested. According to our laws (that's statute 645.7, paragraph three, if you're having trouble finding it), the mayorship can be revoked if, and only if, he or she has died, has lost an election, or has been formally arrested using the lengthy process described in paragraphs four through thirteen. Which, I assure everyone, has yet to happen."

Not a whisker twitched in the assembly hall. All eyes jumped from Mr. Popli to the war council members to Edward the Dung. Most of the citizens wanted Mr. Popli back—Edward had done a miserable job as leader. But none were brave enough to say so.

"Then I hereby arrest you for treason!" said Edward the Dung.

"You can't. I already disbanded the war council."

"WILL SOMEONE ARREST THIS MOUSE?!"

When no one responded, Mr. Popli crawled out of the cereal dish, scaled the podium, and gently nudged the dung beetle out of the way. Edward looked commandingly at one soldier after another, but they all refused to meet his eyes. Defeated, he clomped down from the pedestal.

Mr. Popli reconvened the old council, and they debated for hours over what to do with Huxley. Mr. Popli argued that the juvenile snake ought to be set free, carrying terms of peace back to his mother. Other council members thought they should use him as a hostage to force Colubra to surrender. Others still, those few dark characters loyal to Edward the Dung, thought they ought to nail him to the outer wall.

The moderates prevailed, and plans were formed to send out their entire armada of boats to Colubra's lair the next morning. Till then, Huxley would be a prisoner of war. The juvenile snake sank to the bottom of his cage.

The sun set low on the horizon as the council finalized their plans. "But what if Colubra won't agree to our terms?" asked a sulking Edward the Dung.

"We fight and a lot of us die," said Mayor Popli.

"Unless we can kill her first," added Captain Shift.

Edward the Dung harrumphed. "If we're lucky, both snakes will end up dead."

Chapter 28

Archie pushed and pulled against the oars. "It's the same moon," he told Huxley. "This is the same rowboat. Those are the same stars mapping the way to the same old refrigerator where I found you. I should never have taken you away from your mother. I was wrong about a lot of things. And I hope by getting you home, I can start to fix it."

"Fix it," Huxley hissed in agreement.

"I suppose the worst that could happen is that Colubra eats me for dinner. Unless she then heads to the island and eats all of my friends. Everyone except Edward the Dung, of course, who becomes her new best pal, and they live happily ever after. Yes, that would be the worst that could happen."

Archie had decided to do this alone. After all he'd put poor Mr. Popli through, he couldn't stand to have the mouse join him in another foolish and perilous venture.

When the council broke for dinner, Archie had freed Huxley. It was a simple matter, really. Using the key that Mr. Popli gave to him, he regained access to his workshop. There, he'd built a decoy snake from a length of black rubber tubing and striped it with homemade paint made from sea salt and dandelion flour. Since it was evening and Huxley had been napping, the fake snake, curled in the dim cage, could easily pass for a sleeping Huxley. Then all Archie had to do was create a distraction for the guard, pick the lock on Huxley's cage, and make the switch. Soon they were casting off the rowboat from his secret door.

Familiar rubber duckies bobbed in the ocean current as Archie neared the former mouse colony that had become Colubra's lair. As if sensing his proximity to home, Huxley livened, slithering rapidly from bow to stern and between the shrew's feet.

Well. Here goes. Archie scaled the old refrigerator, recognizing his own claw marks in the moldy grime from his previous visit. He shook like a plastic bag in the wind. Huxley zigzagged up the incline after him.

The still, small voice in Archie's head told him that going forward was a very, very bad idea. For once, he heartily agreed with it. And yet he scuttled in through the ice maker.

The moment Archie stepped a paw inside, he froze, hypnotized by the towering serpent coiled back to strike.

"H-h-hello," he managed. Colubra turned her head curiously to one side.

"I know your scent, thief. Kidnapper. Murderer."

"N-n-no! Not at all! S-s-see? I've brought your son back to you."

Huxley slithered from the shadows of the ice maker behind Archie into the light. Colubra reared up again as Huxley joyfully climbed over and around her. Archie wondered if Huxley might never treat him that way again. But Colubra kept all her attention on the trembling shrew.

"Why?" The serpent loomed over Archie.

"Would you believe it was all an accident? A complete misunderstanding! I saw you with the egg, and I thought—silly me—it was a bird or some other unlucky animal. So, if you look at it from a certain perspective, it was more of a rescue than a kidnapping."

"So you and your islanders took my child, hatched him, and held him captive. But now you're bringing him back to me? So that I might stop attacking you?"

"No!" the shrew said emphatically. "I mean, it was

my fault. The citizens knew nothing about it. I've returned your son in hopes that you'll make peace with us."

The snake's coils writhed back and forth. "You had peace," Colubra hissed. "I found other meals. I allowed your island to prosper. But now you're strong enough to fight against me. And arrogant enough to come into my home and steal what's mine. I have little choice but to put an end to all of you."

That's when Archie realized the depth of his mistake. There would be no peace. No alliance. Just a final, bloody battle in which he would be the first casualty.

"Then I'll fight you." He cast around for a weapon and chose the shattered end of a spear whose previous owner had fared rather poorly.

"If you insist," said Colubra. "But you can't win."

"You've never fought a shrew."

"You're right. Typically, I paralyze and swallow them without a fight."

"No one needs to be paralyzed and swallowed." Mr. Popli cast a long shadow across the lair, creeping over the wreckage of his childhood home. He made his way toward Colubra, Archie, and Huxley. Colubra coiled backward by a mouse length.

"Archibald, you accidentally left without me!"

"Oh, um. My apologies."

"It's a good thing Edward the Dung had the *Abigail* pulled out of the water as evidence, and I had the foresight to have her repaired this afternoon. A bit of tar, some patches—and she's limping along just fine. I was nearly able to catch up with you."

Thank goodness! thought Archie. *If anyone can orchestrate peace between a snake and an island full of snake food, it's good old Mr. Popli.*

"I've come to surrender," said the mouse. Colubra flicked her tongue excitedly.

"You and I have been at war since the day you slithered into my childhood home, taking away everything I knew and loved. You hunted down everyone else. I'm the last mouse alive from this colony. So finish what you started, and then, perhaps, you and the islanders can have peace."

He'd rehearsed the speech a dozen times and delivered it with sincerity and fervor. It was a fine political maneuver. He'd demonstrated humility and a willingness to compromise; now she would see that the islanders were reasonable. That peace could be a possibility, if only both sides would agree. *I hope she doesn't actually take me up on it.*

Colubra lifted herself higher, turning her head

to one side. She struck like a firebolt, snatching Mr. Popli off his feet and retreating with the mouse into the shadows.

Archie scurried for his life.

Chapter 29

No. No. No. No. No. No. No. No. Archie's brain could form no other word. One second, Mr. Popli had been there, doing what Mr. Popli did. Making a speech. Building peace. Fixing Archie's mistakes. And then he was gone—in a flash of scales and fangs and fur. *No. No. No.* The word echoed in his mind as he leapt instinctively aboard the *Abigail*, ignoring his skiff. *No. No. No.* The word pounded in his head in rhythm with the clicks of the engine and chugs of the paddle wheel. *No.* It was his heart's cry of shame as the shrew pedaled the *Abigail* away. Away from Colubra's lair. Away from the island. Away from all the trouble he'd caused.

He pedaled all night, following a cluster of stars he recognized from his charts.

Merri found him the next morning, slumped over the steering mechanism. He stared blankly when she nudged him, eyes glazed from lack of sleep, fur tangled, and skin drawn from the heat.

"Archie, are you okay?"

"No."

"Where's the snake? Belowdecks with Mr. Popli?"

"No."

"Did you take it back to its mother? What did she say? Did she agree to stop attacking the island?"

"No. She said no, Merri. And then she ate Mr. Popli." Saying the words out loud made everything real. Archie's head cleared.

"No!"

"You were right, Merri. She wants all of us gone. Exterminated. I saw her up close. She's faster than a sailfish. Strong as a sea turtle. There's no stopping her. That's why I'm leaving for good."

"You can't."

"I am. And you should come with me. We'll find a new island, start our own civilization."

Archie expected her to refuse, but was unprepared for her response.

"NO—"

"Ow!"

"YOU—"

"Stop it!"

"ARE—"

"That hurts!"

"NOT—"

217

"Please!"

With every word she pecked Archie right on top of his skull. Then she perched next to him, sobbing quietly with her head tucked under her wing.

"Merri, please. What can we do to stop Colubra? To stop the citizens? She's determined to kill us all. We haven't got a spear sharp enough to pierce her scales. There's not a ship in our fleet she can't sink."

"I'm not crying about the citizens. Or the island." The bird sniffled. "I weep for Mr. Popli. He's the only one who ever thought there was a chance for peace. For real community. He spent his whole life working for it. And for what? To be eaten by the same enemy who killed his parents? To see his dream shattered by politicians like Edward the Dung? By cowards like you?" Her words stung more than any peck on his skull.

"I—I don't—I can't—Merri, I don't know what to do! Mr. Popli was the smartest animal I've ever met. He was brave and clever and the citizens listened to him. He saved us from a hundred dangers on our trip. And even *he* couldn't fix this mess. He tried! And now he's slowly digesting in Colubra's stomach. What can I possibly do that he couldn't?"

Merri tilted her head sideways. "You still don't

get it, do you?" The bird gestured out over the ocean. "Look out there. Most of us see trash and hopeless, empty expanses. But you? You look at garbage and see tools and weapons. You stare at the ocean and see farms, food, and highways. Garbage Island wouldn't have existed without Mr. Popli, but it wouldn't have survived without you! And you're the reason I've stayed."

"Oh." Archie had never seen things that way before. He'd never been told he was useful or important. Or, if he had, he'd never believed it. Till now.

And Mr. Popli! Archie blinked. *Even as we disagreed, we created something together—something worth saving.*

Archie felt drained of ideas, though. He sighed. "Merri, I can't fix the mess we're in now."

"But you can show up. You can build. You can help put weapons in the hands of every able-bodied citizen. And you can fight beside me to try to save what Mr. Popli and you built. The island needs you. I need you."

The clouds opened up and rain fell in tiny droplets. Archie watched as they gathered on his snout and rolled down his whiskers. The water bounced off the side of the *Abigail* and snaked along the grooves of the plastic before collecting, drip by drip, in the rain barrels. An idea began to form in the shrew's mind.

"Merri, what did the council decide to do now that they don't have Huxley?"

"Go to war with Colubra. Better to bring the fight to her, they said."

"Can you get back in time to stop the assault? Or slow it down, even for a day?"

"I—I don't know, Archie. Without Mr. Popli, will they listen to either of us? And what good would it do? You said yourself that there's no way we can beat Colubra."

"I was wrong. We may not be able to have peace, but we can win. I've got a plan."

"Simply announcing to the council that Archibald Shrew has another plan will not change their minds. I need something more."

"Tell them . . ." The shrew paused, thinking. He wondered what Mr. Popli might say. "Tell them that I'm bringing a snake of our own. One that's big enough to swallow Colubra whole."

《 》

"This may be the dumbest idea I've ever heard," said Edward the Dung. "Can we vote instead to liberate the island once and for all from this irksome shrew? We're low on ammunition, and his head would make a satisfactory cannonball."

"His plan could work," Merri argued. "And it puts far fewer lives at risk than an open assault on Colubra."

"I want to hear him explain it one more time," said Captain Shift, who had been elected to fill an ominously empty seat on the council.

"Well, the idea is pretty simple. What's the one thing we've made that Colubra has never overcome? Our wall. It's sturdy enough to face the wind. Strong enough to withstand storms. Steady enough to turn back even a bigger fish. Colubra can't get over it or under it or through it. But parts of the wall are hollow."

"And you think we can trap Colubra *inside* the wall?" asked the captain.

Archie was terrified that the citizens wouldn't listen. That they'd rise up against him, or, worse yet, ignore him completely. But a general murmur arose in the crowd. Ears perked up. Brows furrowed. Eyes squinted. All afraid for their lives. All waiting to hear what the shrew had in mind.

"There's a door under the Watchtower that leads in and out of the island through one of those hollow parts of the wall. All we'd have to do is seal off the bottom to make a chamber, then use our ships to lure Colubra back to the island. She chases one of us into the trap. We shut the door behind her. Hopefully, the bait evades her long enough to escape through a small opening we leave toward the interior. She can thrash and flail all she wants. She'll have no way out."

"Then what?" asked Captain Shift. "We go on living with a starving, angry snake in the walls?"

"Then," said Merri, "we do what needs to be done."

Edward the Dung harrumphed a dubious harrumph. "Even if it does work—whoever leads Colubra into this maze is going to be trapped inside the wall with a giant, angry snake! What fool would ever volunteer for such a probable, painful death?"

"I will," said Archie.

Not even Edward could argue with that.

Chapter 30

The plans were made; the trap set. Edward the Dung would lead the fleet within sight of Colubra's lair. They'd use catapults to pelt the door until she came out and gave chase. Then they'd race back to the island, bombarding the water from the walls and leaving an open path to Archie, who would reveal the secret door and lead Colubra through it.

Merri had been tasked with calling out orders from the air to make sure that Colubra followed the path they'd set. But she had second thoughts. "What if she doesn't fall for it? What if she's faster than our ships? What about Huxley?"

"I know. I know," said Archie. "It's a terrible plan, but it's the only one we've got. Unless you'd rather follow Edward the Dung into an all-out assault on Colubra? You could probably choose whether you get to be lunch or dinner."

"Maybe we could just get Colubra to eat Edward?

I'm certain she'd die of indigestion." Merri smiled in a way Archie hadn't seen in quite some time.

"Take care of yourself, Merri. I'm sorry I ever got you into this mess."

"Don't be. You're the only family I've ever known. And family is allowed to be messy. I'm sorry I called you a coward."

Archie ran a paw under her beak, collecting a tear in the fur of his forearm.

"Archibald Shrew, you'd better come out of that wall alive."

《 》

The fleet left through the gate, nearly a dozen rickety barges, rigged with oars, sails, and catapults. All except the *Abigail*. Bringing up the rear, she chugged along under Archie's expert control. Through his looking glass, he spied Edward the Dung at the bow of the lead ship, struggling to keep his balance.

Turning his gaze upward, Archie saw Merri soaring straight along like an arrow, no longer a bird but something else. When she set her mind to battle, she was the fiercest soldier he'd ever seen, warrior and weapon in one.

At the sight of Colubra's lair, the ships formed a wall within firing distance of the old, sunken refrigerator.

Archie heard the sounds of catapults clicking into place and munitions being loaded. They knew they'd never do any damage to the refrigerator—that wasn't the objective. The goal was to make an enormous snake really, really angry.

"FIRE!" came the voice of Edward the Dung.

As one, the ships fired. A barrage of makeshift cannonballs pelted Colubra's lair.

They waited. Nothing. Only the sound of water lapping against the sides of the refrigerator, the boats, the floating garbage.

"FIRE AGAIN!" Once more, the munitions rained down, bouncing off the sides and front door of the flotsam fridge. Merri swooped, looking for signs of Colubra emerging. They fired till nearly all their munitions were gone, never considering that perhaps Colubra wouldn't come out. Or wasn't home.

Finally, the soldiers settled into a stunned silence.

Where is she? Archie asked himself. *What if we missed her? What if she's circled around us and is already at the island? What if we've come to trick her but she's tricked us first? And where is Huxley?*

The shrew waved for Merri and consulted with her on the top deck of the *Abigail*.

"What can you see from the skies?"

"Nothing nearby but some strange weather. She's definitely not in the immediate vicinity. She could be a bit farther away. Or underwater. But—"

"She must be inside!"

"Edward the Dung is about to turn the fleet around and head for home."

"No!"

"Well then, you'd better think of something. Quick."

"I know. I know. Help me think."

"We could sink the fridge," said Merri. "She'd have to come up for air."

"No bombs."

"Could we smoke her out?"

"No matches."

"What do *you* think we should do? Climb in there and drag her out by her tail?"

"Hmmm," said the shrew. "Unconventional, but direct. It might work."

Merri saw a familiar look in the shrew's eye that she didn't like. "Archie, no! I was only joking. It's a terrible idea. Please don't do anything foolish." But it was too late.

"Tell the others to ready the trap! I'm going to climb in there and get her to chase me out."

That's when the spiders attacked.

Chapter 31

They dropped in from the air like a cloud of ash, hundreds of spiders on silken wings.

Merri saw them first and recognized them for what they were—an invasion force. "Look to the skies! Prepare to fight!"

Archie stopped pedaling when he heard. He glanced up, then grabbed his telescope. "Amazing. They've made flying machines!"

While the confused citizens scrambled into formation, Archie marveled at the spiders' ingenuity. Each warrior hung upside down from a woven silk canvas stretched tightly across frames of balsa wood and plastic piping. They shifted their bodies to turn the gliders left and right, to climb into the sky or dive.

When the spiders let go, most of them fell gently onto the ocean. Archie noticed that the tiny hairs on their legs allowed them to scramble across the top of the water. They mounted the sides of the boats and

attacked fearlessly. And like before, any spiders who landed sideways or were hit by salt spray curled up instantly and sank.

The shrew could have watched the graceful gliders for hours, studying the mechanics of their wing construction and estimating the size-to-weight ratios necessary for flight. The things he could do with that silk canvas . . .

Something plopped right next to Archie.

"Merri! Do you see how they release from the gliders? They let out a single strand of silk that acts a bit like a parachute. Oh! Oh my! You're not Merri." The spider who'd landed next to the shrew reared back to attack, claws twitching with the adrenaline of battle. Archie swung the looking glass just as the spider leapt, smacking it over the side of the ship. Three more spiders landed on the *Abigail*, surrounding the shrew. He unstrapped his latest arrow launcher from his back and bared his teeth. The first spider charged. Archie's head whipped sideways. His arrow struck the attacker between its jaws.

The other boats floundered in confusion. They'd prepared for a joint offensive against a single enemy, not a dozen separate battles with hundreds of combatants. Their oversized knives and spears, designed to be effective against a monstrous snake, made clumsy weapons against the smaller, faster attackers.

"Circle the fleet!" Merri shouted from the skies. "Join the boats together and fight as one!" Zipping to and fro and amongst the raining spiders, she shouted orders to the captains and succeeded in herding the ships together.

Merri dove like a falcon, shredding spider gliders with her claws and plucking them from the air with her slashing beak. A hundred spiders fell before her. Like a tornado, she cleared the sky and then turned her wrath toward those left in the water.

Under her command, the citizens fought as one. Many abandoned their weapons, resorting to their natural defenses to fight off the attackers. Lizards snapped with flashing jaws and flung the wounded spiders into the ocean. Armored crickets impaled the arachnids on their spiky exoskeletons. Bombardier beetles sprayed burning hot acid from their hindquarters.

Even Edward the Dung got involved, using his massive strength to roll one of the ship's cannonballs across the deck, squishing spiders under its weight. He laughed as he stormed, making small apologies to the citizens who had to dive out of the way.

Archie, having fought off his initial attackers, pedaled furiously from ship to ship to shoot spiders with his arrow launcher as they cast web lines across the vessels. But the spiders kept coming, fearless, attacking with abandon. Even as their numbers dwindled and defeat was imminent, they regrouped and advanced—clawing, leaping, biting, refusing to surrender.

And then, at last, there were no spiders left.

The sun glared high overhead. Exhausted, the citizens bound up bites and scratches, wiped gore from their bodies, and washed spider guts from the decks of the ships.

Archie and Merri met on the top deck of the *Abigail*. Merri flopped on her feathers, exhausted. Archie stared through his telescope, warily watching the skies.

"Did we get them all?" asked Archie.

"I think so."

"Good. If even one got away to bring news back to their clan . . ."

"We got them all, Archie."

The shrew shifted his looking glass. "I wouldn't be so certain."

Merri's head turned skyward. "Why?"

"Look!"

If the first wave of spider gliders drifted in as a

cloud, the second raged like a tempest. A swarm of shadows on the horizon, they circled and dove without order, without discipline. And they were racing toward Garbage Island.

Chapter 32

Mr. Popli expected it to be warm and damp inside Colubra's belly, yet he shivered in the open air. The pain was also different from what he would have predicted. He'd imagined that digestive juices would burn all over like acid, but only his chest and left arm throbbed from the puncture wounds of the snakebite. Then he wondered why he was wondering about such strange details.

Careful, Popli, he said to himself. *You're starting to think like Archibald!*

Something bristled against the fur on the mouse's face, making his whiskers twitch. The effects of the venom had begun to lessen.

"Stay still," a voice whispered. Or was it a hiss?

"Wh—what happened?"

"Mother supposed you to be my breakfast." Huxley slithered next to the mouse. "I refused. She is . . . displeased."

"I'm sorry. What about Archibald?"

"He's gone."

"Dead?"

"Skedaddled."

"What's to happen with me? With your mother?"

"She desires to speak with you. I expect you have something of significance to say."

"I do." *Or at least, I will*, thought the mouse.

"If she becomes frustrated again, I will be helpless to save you."

Mr. Popli swallowed hard. *Well then, I'd better think of something exceptionally brilliant.*

"She's coming." Huxley slunk back into the shadows. An identical silhouette replaced his, growing larger and larger until it filled Mr. Popli's field of vision.

Colubra flicked the air with her tongue. Neither said anything for a long time.

"What is your name?"

"I am called Mr. Popli, Mayor Popli to some."

"And you know who I am." It was more of a statement than a question.

Mr. Popli thought hard, aware that his life might depend on this exchange of words. If only he could say the right things. If only he could be as quick-witted and clever with the snake as he was with the citizens, he might survive.

"We—we know you as Colubra."

"I have had many names in my lifetime, little mouse. Once I was Beloved of Kaa. Others knew me as She of Flawless Beauty. Others still named me the Striped Queen. There is power in a name, little mouse. You give yourself titles of respect. I am royalty, and yet you dishonor me with the common name you've ascribed to me. So perhaps I will do likewise to you. I could name you Morsel. I could name you Mouthful. I could name you Trespasser, Kidnapper, and Thief."

Mr. Popli rolled on to his good arm and tried to sit up. "Those names are likewise dishonorable. You call me trespasser, but I was born here—not you. You call me kidnapper, but I kept your son alive so he could be returned. You say I'm a thief. But you sleep on a nest made of my clan's possessions. I could name you Slayer of Families. I could call you Nightmare of Noble Animals. I'd dub you Bane of Hope. And, if I could, I would blot your name from the ocean."

Colubra reared up and hissed. "You make me a villain. But I have never killed for the sake of killing— only to survive."

"Look around you! These bones tell the truth. How long did it take you to hunt down the escaping mice? How far did you have to chase them?"

"Lies! When I came upon this lair I was near death. I was lost, far from my hunting grounds in the shallows. I expected to be killed, but instead the mice panicked and fled. I ate an old mouse, one so near death himself he would not run away. He tasted terrible. I waited for them to return. To bring warriors to take back their home. They did not. I healed. I grew stronger. I hunted and fed and filled my lair with the bones of fish and eels and, yes, the occasional islander who wandered too far. But I've only killed to live. I never thought to do more until you kidnapped my son."

This news left Mr. Popli speechless. *Could it be true? But then what happened to the other mice?*

"How can I believe you?"

"You speak of the bones of your family. Look around! You know your species. How many of these remains belong to your clan? How much mammal hair? How many claws? These are the bones of fish too big to swallow. The shells of crabs and crustaceans."

Mr. Popli looked more closely at the scattered animal remains and realized Colubra *could* be telling the truth. But if she wasn't lying, what really happened to his own family? What would have kept them from making it back to the island? Could they still be alive?

"You never attacked my family?"

237

"One mouse looks the same as another to a snake. They all fled. I did not concern myself with where."

Mr. Popli struggled with his emotions. Could she be telling the truth? Had he been wrong all of these years? Was the animosity between them based on a mistaken assumption?

"So where does this leave us? And what happens now?"

"My son refused to eat you, but I am hungry. I suppose that you will have the honor of discovering what comes after this pitiable life. I hope the lingering venom will keep you from feeling too much pain. Still, you may scream if you wish."

Colubra slithered over to the disabled mouse. She dropped her jaw downward from the short bone at the base of her skull, opening a cavernous mouth. Her teeth, angled backward, promised no chance of escape. Once Mr. Popli started down that passage, he would never make it out. The mouse had no more ideas. No clever words or tricks up his fur. Perhaps life could go on for the islanders. Perhaps his family had made it safely to another home. He hoped Colubra was right about the venom.

He closed his eyes, waiting for the piercing pain that would signal the beginning of his end. A moment passed and nothing happened. He squinted one eye open to see that Huxley had reared up between him and Colubra.

Colubra looked more enraged than ever. She was a terror. A demon. A destroyer.

In that moment, Mr. Popli let go of all hope. Huxley would be the first to suffer her wrath. Mr. Popli would follow close behind. And then she'd attack the citizens. All would be death. All would be loss. All would be darkness.

But in this darkness, Huxley began to sing.

> Seven snakes bask in the sun,
> Bright scales, all strong.
> Seven coils, the longest one,
> Sees the nearing storm,
> Moves her six to run.
> Nested snug when rain is come,
> Hatchlings safe and warm.

Colubra tilted her head sideways, mesmerized by the song she'd sung over each brood of her eggs. The song her mother had sung over her. Huxley swayed, and his mother swayed with him. Slowly, slowly, both snakes lowered themselves down until their heads lay on the ground next to Mr. Popli. A lifetime of rage seemed to drain from Colubra's eyes as her every muscle relaxed and she nestled, hypnotized into a moment of peace, next to her son.

Huxley eyed the enemies each in turn. "If I suggested an alternative solution, would you both consider it?"

Chapter 33

The storm of spider gliders billowed toward the island.

Merri raced ahead of them.

She landed in time to warn the citizens, but only just. A guard sounded the bell three times, the signal for all noncombat citizens to lock themselves inside their homes. Before the echoes finished reverberating through the metal and glass and plastic, spiders began to drop from the sky.

Members of the Order who had remained on the island, expecting a snake but facing a spider invasion, panicked. They would have been overrun if not for Merri, who sprinted tirelessly from company to company, squawking orders. "You lizards! Circle up in groups of three! Crickets! Get behind the beetles! Aim for their eyes, not their legs!"

She stopped to fight only when she heard cries for help. A family of carrion beetles, cut off in their flight to get indoors, cowered on the edge of a swimming pool noodle. The mother flashed her wings menacingly at the spiders blocking their escape, able to keep only a spider width between the attackers and her infants. The spiders, sensing her panic, gathered and advanced. They lunged at the children, getting closer on one side every time the mother lashed to the other. It was a practiced tactic, one they'd used to fell many a family.

But the spiders were unprepared for Merri, and she'd only gotten better at killing them. She landed behind their lines, stabbing with her beak. She snuffed out a spider with every peck, flitting up into the sky to dodge a leaping enemy here or throw an eight-legged attacker there. The smallest, juiciest ones she gobbled up. In a minute she'd cleared a path for the beetle family. They scurried inside their home and Merri rejoined the fray.

Meanwhile, Archie attempted to murder Edward the Dung.

At the sight of the second wave of spiders, the dung beetle had lowered his head solemnly and offered condolences to the poor souls on Garbage Island. "We can only honor their memories by taking our ships in search of safer waters." Edward was leader of the citizens' armada, and the other boats began to follow.

Chasing the spiders in the *Abigail*, it had taken Archie several moments to notice that the rest of the ships had not joined his pursuit. That they were, in fact, running away. They'd lost precious minutes by the time he'd maneuvered the houseboat alongside the lead warship and scurried up to the helm.

As Edward began to explain his cowardly command, he caught a familiar gleam in Archie's eye. In fact, the dung beetle swore that he'd seen that expression on Merri, but only when she was getting ready to fight.

The shrew scooped up the beetle in one paw and swung him over the side of the ship.

"We're going back," said Archie.

"It's hopeless! Insanity! Suicide! Besides, I'm in charge! You have to do what I say!" A dorsal fin sliced through the water. Edward tried to roll himself up and away from the waves, but he could reach neither the shrew nor the side of the boat.

"We'll do it your way, then," said Archie.

Edward shrieked, expecting to be dropped into the ocean. But the shrew held firm. (To be perfectly honest, he may have allowed his grip to slide, but only a little.)

"I hereby relieve Edward the Dung from his duty as captain of this fleet. For cowardice. For dereliction of duty." None of the soldiers on deck moved or said a word.

"I know you all took an oath," the shrew continued, looking around. "You made a promise to set out from

the island whenever others were in danger. And you knew, going out, that you might not make it home. So today you've kept your promise. You've set out. You've faced danger. However, if we don't make it home today, we'll lose everything we've worked for. I know I'm not in charge. But if I were, I'd have us all sail full speed to protect our home."

Captain Shift, the leopard gecko who'd threatened to sink them just the day before, stepped forward, spear in hand. A half dozen other soldiers stood by her side. Had Archie gone too far, pushed too hard against the protocol of the island? Edward the Dung offered no help, merely wriggling and squealing in Archie's paw. The shrew finally set the beetle back on the warship's deck.

Captain Shift raised herself up to her full height, a shrew and a half taller than Archie. "Every one of us has a family back there. We only volunteered for the Order of the Silver Moon to keep them safe. You lead us. We'll follow you, Admiral Archibald."

"My name is Archie."

Archie had always thought leadership was giving orders and making others do what you wanted. But this—this was something altogether different. He felt weak and strong at the same time—weak because he was powerless on his own, yet mighty because he had earned the trust of his comrades.

"Let's go home!" shouted Archie. A roar of approval met his ears. He boarded the *Abigail* and chugged toward the island at the head of the fleet.

They made good time, and soon Garbage Island loomed larger. But now another shape, long and low, rose up between them and home. Archie adjusted his looking glass.

"What is it?" Captain Shift called from the next ship.

"It's Colubra."

Snakespit! In the melee with the spiders, they'd forgotten about the snake. The shrew's hopes plummeted. They'd barely survived the first spider assault. How could they possibly overcome an even bigger spider force *and* a giant, raging snake, both obsessed with their annihilation?

"Prepare for battle! Ready the catapults!" Behind Archie, the sounds of rustling animals mixed with the steady rhythm of ocean waves. Paws and tails sent signals to the other ships in the fleet.

Archie watched through his telescope as Colubra slithered toward them. "WAIT! What's the word for stop? BELAY THAT ORDER! WEAPONS DOWN!" Huxley swam beside his mother. Together they towed a tiny vessel, no bigger than a butter dish. A white flag fluttered. A paw raised in a gesture of peace.

"IT'S MAYOR POPLI!"

Edward the Dung argued that it must be a trap, that Colubra had probably killed Mr. Popli and brought him along as bait to lure them all in. Captain Shift ignored the beetle and asked Archie for his orders.

"Captain, I know this is going to sound a bit crazy, but I don't think Colubra is here to fight us. Let me run ahead with the *Abigail* and see what's what. If anything goes wrong, I want you to go straight to the island and fall in with Merri and the rest of the Order."

"Yes, Admiral."

"Captain, you've taken more risks on me than I deserve. I won't forget it."

"You proved yourself to me when you stood up to Edward."

"Yes. Well. About Edward the Dung . . ."

"If he tries anything else, I'll put him in the catapult and pull the trigger myself."

The two waved to each other. Then Archie raced toward Mr. Popli and the slithering predators who swam with him. The fleet followed at a distance, ready to split up and circle toward the island should the snakes show any signs of aggression. Which, based on the islanders' beliefs about Colubra, was almost certain.

The reunion with Mr. Popli and Huxley would have been more joyous for Archie if not for the threat of imminent death from an army of spiders and the fear of an even more immediate death from a giant, shrew-eating snake. Colubra circled the *Abigail* as Archie helped Mr. Popli and Huxley onto the top deck.

"Mr. Popli—"

"Archibald, you'll never believe it!" the mouse interrupted. "When Colubra bit me—bruised ribs and some puncture wounds, no more—I thought I was going to be eaten, but then Huxley refused to eat me, which made Colubra rather cross. (She'd prefer we call her Bright Scales from now on, by the by.) And then we had the longest talk and I made her really, really angry, and Huxley saved me again! And now we're to have peace! At long last, Archibald!"

"So you're not here to kill us?" Archie addressed the giant snake.

Bright Scales shook her head. "Not today."

"Not ever, if we can manage to keep our end of the bargain," said Mr. Popli. "Isn't it wonderful?"

"Yes . . . But the spiders—" said Archie.

"Don't worry about the spiders. They're leagues away. They'll never find us."

"They found us. They're attacking the island right now."

"Archibald Shrew! Why didn't you say so?!"

"Because you were going on and on. I never know how to stop you when you're doing that."

"Is there a plan?"

"Fight and probably die."

"That's not a very good plan."

"It's all we have."

"What if we had a snake on our side?"

"And a second snake," said Huxley.

"Neither of whom have eaten in days," added Bright Scales.

"Well, now. That could certainly open up some possibilities."

Chapter 34

As the sun set, spider gliders circled Garbage Island, keeping watch on the fleet gathering near the gate on its southernmost tip. They'd overtaken the island, sending all of the citizens and members of the Order into their homes to hide. Now it was a siege, and they only had to wait.

Merri began to spread the word amongst the islanders—calling through one barricaded door after another—that the snake was on their side, that the fleets were back, and that they had a plan to get rid of the spiders. Each time she checked in with the fleet, she brought small containers of oil from the storehouses. They'd need it if anyone got caught in the sticky spider silk.

Meanwhile, Captain Shift volunteered for the dangerous task of undoing the trap that had been set for Colubra. Their plan was essentially the same one they'd had before—except this time instead of trapping the carnivorous snake in the wall, they were going to let her loose in the island. This meant someone had to get through the wall, past the spiders, and then remove nails and move all of the heavy garbage they'd used to block the exit from the secret passage. Captain Shift hefted a spear up on one shoulder.

"You'll need some extra muscle," said Edward the Dung, looking rather sheepish. "I was a coward. And I don't deserve to be a part of this mission. But I can still push better than anyone. Will you let me help?"

"There's hope for you yet, Mr. Dung. You're in!" said Captain Shift. "What weapon can we give you?"

"Oh, I won't be much good in a fight. Too slow for a weapon. But at least I've got armor. I'm sure they'll kill you long before they get to me."

"Now there's a comforting thought."

‹ ›

In the dead of night, not a single spider noticed the gecko and beetle sneak silently onto the island. None observed them enter the secret passage in the wall. None overheard Edward's muffled profanity when he got stuck in the shrew-sized hole intended for Archie. And not a worry crossed a tiny arachnid brain when Captain Shift finally wrestled him through, nor when

251

the two stumbled right into a giant patch of sticky web.

The trap was guarded by the biggest spider they'd ever seen. It was snoring loudly.

Edward stifled the shriek rising up in his throat.

"Don't move!" hissed the gecko. "Archie was right about the sticky web. This could get bad very quickly if we struggle. Which leg is the oil pouch tied to?"

"Back right. I'll see if I can move it toward your hand."

"Careful! You're shaking the web!"

"Do you want the oil or not?!" The giant spider yawned and twitched. The pair stood still as starlight till the spider stopped moving.

"Hurry," Captain Shift whispered. "And let's get out of here before we wake her up."

Edward and Captain Shift poured the oil on any body part stuck in the web, slowly freeing themselves.

"What about your spear?" asked Edward. The weapon lay back across the sticky web, firmly stuck and beyond reach.

"We'll have to make do without. Unless you want me to toss you back over there to get it."

Edward declined.

"Shall we get to work?" asked Captain Shift. "Most of the spiders should be dozing like this big guy. If we're lucky."

"Since when were we lucky?" Edward asked, tripping over a bent wire. He nearly collided with a tower of stacked bottle caps that would have fallen with a clamor. Captain Shift caught him just in time.

"There's a first time for everything." The gecko turned, her tail swishing past the stack of bottle caps with just enough breeze to send it toppling right onto the giant spider's head. Hissing and spitting, the spider shook off the fallen bottle caps and glared at the two with eight menacing eyes.

"He looks grumpy," Edward commented.

"You would be, too, if you'd been woken up by heavy things crashing onto your head," said the gecko. She looked for a place to run, but she was trapped between the spider and its web. "Get ready! It can't possibly handle both of us."

The spider lunged. Unfortunately, Edward had already fled. Cursing, Captain Shift jumped to one side and scoured for a new weapon. She found the broken end of a plastic fork with three remaining tines. The utensil was awkward, too clumsy to stab or parry. But she swung at the spider with the fork and slashed with her tail, using the weapon also as a shield when the predator leapt and snapped.

The captain had fought and killed dozens of spiders when they swarmed the armada, but never one this

large. It sidled easily away from her attacks and lashed out with hooked claws on thick legs, trying to catch the gecko to draw her toward its deadly fangs.

Pinned against a rusty spray can, fangs nearly at her belly, Captain Shift struggled to keep the spider at bay between the broken tines of the fork. Just when the gecko thought she'd reached the end of her luck, a battered cricket ball came crashing past her, rolling over the giant spider with a satisfying squish. Edward the Dung emerged from the shadows, grinning.

"You know you could have just as easily crushed me with that thing."

"I'm a dung beetle. I roll things. I'm rather accurate."

"Well then, thank you, I suppose, for . . . rolling so accurately."

Now aware of the sticky web traps as well as the oversized spiders that guarded them, the comrades set to work clearing the debris that blocked the secret entrance. As quietly as they could, Edward rolled away bottles, tins, and driftwood while Captain Shift worked on removing the nails one by one.

"Shh," hissed Edward. "You make more noise than a sea lion!"

"I'm not the one bungling around like a crocodile in a crab trap!" replied the gecko.

In reality, the pair worked rather quietly and quickly. By the time the stars began to fade and the sky shifted toward its deep purple, premorning hues, a path was clear for the citizens to retake their island.

Chapter 35

The *Abigail* sat low in the water, heavy-laden, with spider guts and webbing adding further blemishes to its severely damaged exterior. Mr. Popli grimaced at the condition of his beloved houseboat, but it was the least of his worries.

A hundred members of the Order of the Silver Moon pushed and elbowed for breathing room inside the hull. Overcrowded and grumpy from being cramped so close together all night, they waited for the order to attack. The other ships in the fleet carried only the wounded. Like a toothless tuna, they had no weapons—their job was to hold the spiders' attention on the other end of the island.

"There!" said Mr. Popli. "They've done it!" He handed the looking glass to Archie.

The shrew peered through it and saw Captain Shift waving a bit of orange thread, the prearranged signal that their mission was a success and all was ready for them to proceed.

"It's about time," said the shrew. "Now let's take back our island!"

"Careful," replied the mouse. "You're beginning to sound a bit like me."

After ferrying the small army through the secret door, Mr. Popli and a skeleton crew navigated the houseboat back toward the rest of the armada. With its new team of pilots, the *Abigail* spat and jumped and stuttered along a winding course around the island. "Well, of course it's hard to pedal. Put some muscle in it! That's the brake! Not the steering! No, no, no! You pull right to go left . . ."

The plan was simple. Use the element of surprise and secret serpent weapons to clear the island from one end to the other. Once they'd secured the badlands and the inhabited area, Bright Scales and Huxley would take the lagoon, plucking the spiders from the surface as the Order of the Silver Moon drove the remaining combatants toward them.

Archie had spent the night making dozens of weapons, from more arrow launchers to blowguns to handheld saltwater cannons. When Captain Shift asked about the salt water, he'd explained his theory that ocean water was poisonous to the spiders.

"The first time we fought them, I noticed that the injured ones who couldn't walk on the water curled up almost as soon as salt water touched their exoskeletons. It even explains why they built their homes so high up on their island."

"So if we're about to be overwhelmed, all we have to do is jump in the ocean?" the spotted gecko asked.

"As a last resort, of course," said Archie. "They can still capture us in nets and webbing, but I don't think they'll touch anyone until the salt water dries off. It could give us extra minutes or even hours depending on how sensitive they are to the salt."

"And what if we jump in the water and your theory is wrong?" asked Edward the Dung accusingly.

"Hmm . . . In that case I suppose that we increase our chances of being eaten in one big gulp by a fish, without of course decreasing the odds of having the spiders turn our insides into a venomous soup."

"Oh."

Most of the troops were now armed, and they waited in the wall for Merri to signal that the distraction had begun.

"Snakespit! Sorry, Colubra—I mean Bright Scales." Archie fumbled on his words. "Where is Merri?"

The signal was supposed to be the sound of glass

beads clanging down the steps of the Watchtower, released by Merri as soon as the ships on the north end of the island began their mock assault. The ships had already volleyed a dozen cannonballs at spiders on the gate, afraid to send more because of the citizens who might still be confined indoors. But Merri failed to signal that everything was going according to plan because, as usual, it wasn't.

This was so much easier the first time, thought Merri, flitting backward into a dive. This time the spiders were prepared to do battle with a bird, even one of Merri's ferocity and savvy. She narrowly missed a net of sticky web that two gliders carried between them before sending the pair spiraling down in their own tangled gob of webbing. *Two down. Ten to go.*

That's when Merri noticed that these gliders, and the spiders that piloted them, seemed bigger than the ones they'd faced yesterday. Another one shot past her, spraying sticky web onto her wing. *Definitely bigger! The advance guard must've been their youngest and weakest.* She shook her wing but the webbing would not come off. *Another hit like that and I won't be able to fly.*

Merri zipped down as close to the water as she dared, a half dozen gliders swooping after her. She could beat the spider gliders in a sprint, but they flew tirelessly and relentlessly, gaining on her every time she slowed down. She saw a perfect wave ahead. *Closer. Closer!* The gliders nipped at her tail feathers. *Almost! Just a little closer!*

She swooped under the crest of the wave and turned upward, shooting like an arrow straight through the spray and out the other side. The spider gliders were not so lucky. Five of them crashed straight into the wave; the last one pulled up just in time, narrowly missing the fate of its comrades.

Looking back, Merri thought, *I'll bet they never saw that one coming.* Then she flew straight into an unfurled net of sticky web that was waiting for her, stretched between a pair of gliders. She crashed into the ocean, dragging the two gliders with her into the water.

《 》

"Excuse me, Bright Scales," said Archie to the snake. "I . . . I realize that everyone is rather famished, but it's much worse for all of us when we hear you say it. Your voice echoes in the chamber, and it's a bit unsettling, you know, to hear the, um, former nemesis of our people, the nightmare of our children's stories, mumbling about how hungry she is. I imagine you can understand."

"I promised not to eat any of you," Bright Scales

replied testily. "But if I don't eat soon I will expire. It's the way of snakes."

And so, seeing no alternative, Archie decided not to wait for Merri's signal. The army crept out of the passage and onto the island so Bright Scales could have breakfast.

After the first few spiders they encountered, most of the members of the Order had forgotten their own hunger.

"Crunchy," exclaimed Bright Scales. "And chewy at the same time."

"With a flavor explosion right in the middle!" added Huxley. "Oooh! Mother! The small ones are sweeter!"

Edward the Dung turned greener than normal, as though he might release his breakfast back into the wild.

The army moved stealthily across the island, securing the wall as they went. Within every group, one soldier carried a small container of the oil Merri had brought—just in case they got caught in sticky web.

"Nice shot, Archie," said Huxley as another spider fell from the ramparts. The juvenile snake slithered up a mound of trash to retrieve the fallen spider and Archie's arrow.

"We won't be able to stay hidden much longer," said

Captain Shift. "I can only hope we've secured enough of the island to keep them from surrounding us. How are our two secret weapons feeling?"

"Excellent," said Huxley.

"Strong," said Bright Scales.

"We'll finish clearing the badlands shortly. Then we'll be within sight of the lagoon. That's where all the families will be holed up and where the majority of the spider army should be lurking. With any luck you'll have a straight shot into the lagoon. You lead the charge; we'll follow and trap the spiders between us and you. As long as nothing unforeseen happens, that should be the end of it."

They scrambled over the last crest of the badlands to confront the unforeseen. Archie peered through the looking glass. Across the lagoon, Mr. Popli and more than a dozen other citizens hung from the gate, covered in sticky web. *The ships! They've been captured!* thought the shrew. *But where is Merri?*

Then he turned his gaze downward. There, covering the ground like fallen ash, more spiders than he could count scrambled and clawed and climbed in all directions.

Chapter 36

At the edge of the badlands, Archie's remaining citizen army took cover wherever they could find it—behind broken bottles, under sun-scorched grocery bags, or inside empty takeout containers. Archie conferred with Captain Shift. The best plan he could imagine required five times as many fighters, a dozen functional coil-powered engines, and two empty jars with holes poked in the lids. He didn't even have the lids.

Captain Shift offered no better ideas. "I thought we'd nearly won, but we've barely made a dent!"

"A dozen snakes couldn't eat that many," said Bright Scales.

"And the prisoners won't have much time," Archie muttered. "It may be too late already."

"It's *definitely* not too late to run away," suggested Edward the Dung.

Rapping a fist against his head, Archie tried to connect the dots. *Think, Archie. Think!* This was *his* island. He knew it backward and forward. They hadn't yet been spotted, so they still had the advantage of surprise. He had a workshop brimming with tools and useful things plus anything they could scavenge from the badlands. "What are spiders afraid of?"

"The same things all animals fear," said Captain Shift. "Starvation. Bad weather. Predators."

"Brilliant thinking," said Edward unhelpfully. "And here we've handed them an island overflowing with prey, protected against the weather, and perfectly secure from just about anything that would want to swim up or climb over. We may as well roll ourselves in seasoning and surrender."

"You're right about one thing," said Archie. "We can't beat them by land or sea. We need our own air force!"

"And I suppose you've got one in that satchel of yours," Edward chided.

But the shrew's mind was already churning, calculating times and distances and materials. At last he looked at Bright Scales with a lopsided grin. "Maybe not a whole air force. But what if we had a dragon?"

Bright Scales reared back, turned her head sideways, and considered the shrew. "I don't think I'm going to like this idea."

Captain Shift hastily prepared a small, elite rescue squad to free the captured citizens. Archie directed the majority of the troops back at the Watchtower.

"Add more sticky web to the second joint on the left wing! Careful not to get it on your hands. Are the seams holding? Good! Good! Reginald, how's the harness coming along? Excellent! Janice, how's work on the bell tower? Marvelous!"

"I don't suppose we could still attempt to offer terms of peace?" asked Bright Scales.

"The spiders aren't much for talking, in my experience," said Archie. "Besides, haven't you ever wondered what it's like to fly?"

"Yes. And I imagined that I would not like it at all."

"Oh. Well. That's unfortunate."

« »

"So we're supposed to run and scream?" asked Edward. "I'm quite confident I can do that." From the edge of the badlands between the Watchtower and Merri's perch, the rescue squad waited for their signal.

"This is the craziest idea that shrew has ever had," replied Captain Shift. "There is absolutely no way it's going to work."

And then came a roar. A hollow, rumbling tone that shook the ground and made Captain Shift stumble toward Edward. Every arachnid eye turned toward the sound. There, rising from the top of the Watchtower, the spiders and citizens beheld a great winged serpent.

Its body writhed. Its jaws snapped, fangs glistening in the sun. Huge bat-like wings cast an ominous shadow across the badlands. A monster of legend had arrived on Garbage Island, and spiders and citizens alike trembled.

"Oh my," said Captain Shift. "This may work after all. CHARGE!" Her troops scrambled out of the badlands and rushed the spider army. The ground shook again. Spiders faltered and fell. Between the earth-shaking rumble, the vision of the winged beast, and the surprise of the troops charging with saltwater cannons, the spiders began to turn and retreat.

Pack instinct and fear took over. Like a wave growing in size, the spider army fled before Captain Shift. Her battalion of ten routed hundreds of spider warriors. Out of the turnip gardens, past the lagoon, up and over the ramparts they raced, slipping and sliding down the oiled wall and into the ocean. Some curled up and sank when the salt stung their exoskeletons like acid. Most scrambled across the water onto the emptied warships from the islanders' armada. They rowed. They sailed. The ones who couldn't make it onto a ship scurried on their own legs. Anything to get away from the terror that plagued this island.

Archie, Huxley, and the rest of the soldiers not tending to Bright Scales joined the pursuit. As they reached Captain Shift and her troop at the top of the wall, they laughed. Their island was free of spiders.

"We did it!" Archie squealed, hugging the larger gecko around the middle. "They're gone!"

"Yes, sir, but—"

"But what? They're swimming away like frightened minnows!"

"They've taken Merri."

"No!"

"We rescued the other prisoners, including Mayor Popli, but Merri fought so hard when she was captured that they never could pull her up the wall. They finally got her tied down on the *Abigail* and they're dragging it behind them. We'd have given chase, but we haven't got a skiff left in the fleet. We've got no way to go after her."

"Oh, yes we do. We've got a dragon."

《 》

Archie could still see the fleeing spider ships in the distance through his looking glass, but the setting sun promised he'd lose Merri for good if he didn't hurry.

"Quickly!" The last belt snapped into place on the harness. The shrew pulled on the left and right ropes that maneuvered each wing.

"Do you really think it will fly?" asked Captain Shift.

"I had the idea for these wings the second I saw the

spider gliders," said Archie. "I calculated for lift and weight ratios and motility. Of course there's no way it would have ever flown Bright Scales. But me? I'm the perfect size. I think."

"That doesn't really answer my question," said the gecko, tightening a strap on the contraption. "My guess is we'll be scraping you off the bottom of the Watchtower."

"Well, I suppose we'll know in a moment."

And with that, Archie leapt.

Chapter 37

The spiders thought the monster was giving chase. They redoubled their rowing and trimmed their sails and cowered in the hulls of the boats. Archie spotted Merri. Her head poked out of the tangle of sticky web with which they'd trapped her. She was breathing. *Thank goodness!* thought the shrew.

Archie wished he could take time to relish the glider. The design marked a beautiful fusion of spider ingenuity with his own. He'd needed more than a dozen of the salvaged spider gliders to construct the wings, and he doubted he'd ever find enough of the super-strong silk weave to make another set. It was too bad the wings weren't likely to survive to be used for other inventions. *But there are far more important things than my inventions*, he thought. And then he dive-bombed the enormous glider into the stern of the houseboat that held his captive friend.

The spiders had abandoned ship as soon as they

saw the shadows of those wings racing toward them. They were taking no chances after what they'd seen and heard and felt on the island. All except one ancient, grizzled, gray-haired spider with seven legs and a stub. Having failed to conquer the island, he didn't want to return to his clan in defeat and even welcomed death.

He waited in the shadows as Archie struggled up the side of the ship. His eight eyeballs shook with fury when he realized they'd been tricked. Then he crept carefully behind Archie, cautious of the weapon the shrew had tucked under one arm. Step by step, he inched his way to where Archie poured a container of oil over the sticky web that entangled the yellow bird.

The spider prickled with delight as Merri's expression shifted from relief to terror, recognizing the danger too late. Satisfaction filled him to know that she watched as his fangs bored into the shrew's back, injecting every drop of poison hatred he had. For his clan's loss. For the shrew's deception. For his own disgrace. Empty of venom, he leapt past the shrew and toward Merri. Something stopped him in midair.

The old spider wondered at the pain as he noticed the dull end of Archie's arrow launcher protruding from his abdomen, Archie still holding on to its other end. Falling to the deck, his final thought was one of relief. At least he'd died in battle. At home the new spider queen would've killed him in a far more painful manner. With one last twitch, the ancient spider expired.

Merri flailed against her bonds, finally able to free herself from the no-longer-sticky web. She could hardly move, much less fly, but she kicked the spider into the sea and crawled to nestle her friend in her wings.

"Oh, Archie! You great, terrible nincompoop!" She wept large, egg-shaped tears.

The shrew managed a weak grin and then, taking shallow breaths, closed his eyes.

As the sun began to set, a pair of serpent heads rose up on either side of the boat.

"We've come to fulfill our promise," said Bright Scales. "The spiders have been driven away. For now. Your ships are gone, but your island is safe. Let us bring you home." Huxley and Bright Scales each took a towline in their jaws and swam the ship back to the island, through the gate, and into the lagoon. They ferried the vessel toward the assembly hall, now a makeshift hospital for the many wounded. At the prow of the ship, Merri stood vigil over the only family she'd ever known. She begged the stars to let him stay with her.

As they skimmed along the waterway, a few citizens cheered. But more than a few recoiled from the snakes. Some gasped. Others murmured curses when the serpents passed by. With every corner they turned, Merri could feel the eyes upon them. If she was an outsider before, how would the citizens treat her now that she kept the company of snakes? She decided that she no longer cared.

When they arrived at the assembly hall, Merri told the snakes, "We can take him from here." Strong claws took hold of the towlines and small animals jumped aboard the ship.

"Then we leave you," said Bright Scales. "And we hold you and your Mr. Popli responsible for protecting this alliance of peace. I suggest you treat it as if your life depends on it."

Merri nodded. Bright Scales and Huxley dove underwater and out through the gate, away from the gaping mouths and gawking eyes of the citizens.

Chapter 38

Being strung up in a spider web for hours, fur soaked through with seawater, while still recovering from a snakebite, had taken a toll on Mr. Popli. They'd cut him down from the wall and ferried him to a bed in the assembly hall. He regained consciousness a day later, weak and disoriented. It was two more days till he was well enough for visitors.

Nurses escorted Captain Shift to the mouse's bedside. She appeared tired and haggard, evidence of hard-fought battles and the continuing aftermath.

"You have to tell me *everything*, Captain. These medics absolutely refuse to speak to me about the invasion."

"Sorry, Mayor. That was on my order. I wanted to tell you all the news myself, and the nurses wouldn't let me near till today. They're quite insistent, those nurses— especially the wasp who works in the mornings. She threatened to sting me!"

Mr. Popli laughed. "I know the one you're talking about. I wish we'd had her during the invasion!"

"Apparently we did! The other nurses claim she fought off a dozen spiders while leading families to safety."

"I can just imagine that! But did the plan work? Are the citizens all safe?"

"We lost a number of citizens. The crickets were hit hard. So were the mud daubers. The larger animals seemed to fare better."

"Merri? Archibald? Huxley? Are they okay?"

"They're alive . . ."

"And Colubra—I mean Bright Scales?"

"Unscathed, but reclusive. She's gone back to her lair and hasn't been seen. Huxley spends the days here and the nights there. He says his mother still believes the islanders are angry with her."

"Are they?"

"Of course. There have been too many losses over the years—and too much anger. It was only days ago we thought *she* was the invader. Those wounds won't heal quickly. But there are also many who speak of her valor during the invasion, especially among the Order."

Mr. Popli thought about his own wounds from Bright Scales, both old and new. Their recent talks had been uneasy, but enlightening. He was no longer convinced that snakes were enemies and monsters. Perhaps they were noble, misunderstood creatures with whom peace was a genuine possibility. *Perhaps I can believe she spared my family.*

"We'll have to see how we can ensure the peace with her. But tell me about defeating the spiders. Did you see how well our distraction worked? We catapulted a few volleys at the gate, and in what seemed like only an instant, spider gliders were everywhere. Of course they overwhelmed us immediately. But we jumped into the water. And then there were nets and webs and before we knew it they had us hanging upside down from the gate."

"We had some tricky moments ourselves," the gecko replied. "We had no idea how many spiders had come. Or how big they would be!" She went on to explain Archie's quick thinking and the plan that finally worked.

"He turned Bright Scales into a dragon?! Oh, I wish I could have seen it! I did hear the terrible roaring sound that shook the ground though. How did you make it? We all thought a whale had come to swallow the island!"

"Another of Archie's ideas. His secret passage was mostly sealed off. He had us stop up the end, which we'd opened for the snakes, and the belfry as well.

Then, we rang the bell harder than it's ever been rung. The vibrations had nowhere to go except down the Watchtower and through the passage, growing as they went. That's what shook the island. And when the sound escaped through holes and crevasses—well, it sounded a bit monstrous."

"Amazing! And the spiders?"

"Gone. For now. Based on the direction they came from and which way they retreated, Merri thinks she knows where their island is. It's farther than she can fly in a day, but the Order of the Silver Moon patrols that direction and hasn't seen any sign."

The gecko described how the spider army fled, kidnapping Merri, and how Archie had used the dragon wings to rescue her.

"You mean the wings worked? He flew? Leave it to Archibald to design fake wings that actually work. Will he be able to visit soon?"

"Sir, he's . . . he's not well."

"What do you mean, *not well?*"

"A spider got him, sir, while he was saving Merri. It pumped him so full of poison we thought he'd never wake up. He did, but . . ."

"But what?"

"He's gone blind, sir."

"Oh, Archibald!" The mouse was silent a moment before whispering, "And Merri?"

"I don't think a giant squid could take her down. She's fine, but won't leave his side. I hardly have the heart to send her on patrol."

Chapter 39

A week later, and much sooner than his nurse would have preferred, Mr. Popli went to visit Archie. Truthfully, the wasp had told the mouse he couldn't leave under *any* circumstances. And so, in the middle of the morning while she was busy with other patients, Mr. Popli broke out of the hospital.

As he hobbled down the airplane stabilizer toward Archie's workshop, he relished the sounds of waves and wind mixed with the buzzes and chirps of citizens.

While Mr. Popli had been confined to the hospital, the mouse's mind had been brewing with plans and ideas. He couldn't wait to tell the shrew all about them.

He knocked on the door to Archie's workshop.

"I'm an invalid and I'm not getting up! You can leave pies on the windowsill!"

"Archibald?"

"Mayor Popli? Come in! Come in! Merri, look who it is!"

Mr. Popli hobbled into Archie's workshop. He was relieved to see that Archie had already gained some weight. He must have been receiving a lot of pies indeed. After hugging his friend, Mr. Popli immediately busied himself making tea as they filled each other in on all the missing pieces from their adventures.

While they talked, Archie moved about his workshop with paws outstretched, using his whiskers and tail to sense for walls, chairs, and cabinets. If he was bothered by his condition, he didn't show it at all.

Eventually, Merri left to attend to some overdue business with the Order of the Silver Moon. She promised to be back in time for dinner. And since Mr. Popli was hiding from his nurse, the mouse volunteered to stay till she returned. There were many pies to be eaten and all the dandelion tea they could drink.

"So what happens now, Mayor Popli?"

"Actually, it won't be *Mayor* Popli any longer. I'm stepping down."

"What? Why hasn't anyone told me?"

"Nothing's official yet. But it will be. As soon as the new division of the Order is up and running."

"Now that I *have* heard about."

"They're calling themselves Archie's Shrew Seekers."

Archie fell silent for a moment. "Thank you for

doing this, Mr. Popli. I've dreamt about something like it ever since I lost my family."

"I should be thanking you. And asking your pardon, Archie. You heard what Bright Scales told me. My family could be out there, too. My whole colony. This division of the Order will search for our families. I plan to join them."

"Then so will I. When do we start?"

The mouse hemmed and hawed for a moment, unsure of how to say what he hoped the shrew already understood. "We'll get you involved just as soon as your eyesight comes back." *If it comes back.*

"Ridiculous! I don't need to see to help you plan an adventure!"

"Yes, but we'll need your eyes on every inch of the ship and every detail of the voyage. That's why we're waiting for you to get better."

That answer seemed to pacify the shrew. "But you won't leave without me?"

"We'd never dream of it."

"Good." The shrew thought for a moment. "Who do you think will be mayor in your place?"

"It's too soon to say. Captain Shift, perhaps? That is, of course, if everyone's number one choice isn't at all interested."

"Who? Not Edward the Dung, I hope."

"No, I'm talking about someone who demonstrated real leadership during the invasion. A hero."

"You mean Merri, of course! I'll bet she took out half the spiders all by herself!"

"Not Merri . . ."

"Mrs. Toad?"

"Old Mrs. Toad? The one who eats plastic berries?!"

"I heard she swallowed a lot of spiders during the invasion . . . But I give up! Who?"

"You, Archie! Your quick thinking, your selfless defense of the island and the families, the way you led the Order and repelled the invasion—you'd be elected mayor in a heartbeat."

"Oh!" The shrew felt a sudden warmth in his chest that had nothing to do with the tea.

Just then a loud knock at the door interrupted them.

"You can leave it on the windowsill!" called the mouse, which set both him and Archie to laughing.

"MAYOR POPLI! WE HAVE TURNED THIS ISLAND UPSIDE DOWN LOOKING FOR YOU!"

"Snakespit," said Mr. Popli. "The nurse! I don't suppose you have any more secret passages or hidden doors, do you?"

"You have no idea," replied Archie with a grin.

Author's Note

A vortex of floating trash swirls in the Pacific Ocean. As I learned more about it, I wondered, What if terrestrial animals got marooned there? Other questions followed: What kind of animals? What would they eat and drink? How could they live side by side? To satisfy my curiosity, I wrote *Garbage Island*. My hope is not to lay blame for the existence of the Great Pacific Garbage Patch, but to inspire a new generation of intrepid geniuses who, like Archibald and Mr. Popli, see the trash as a puzzle we can solve together.

Acknowledgments

I'd never be a published author without years of honing my craft through the Society of Children's Book Writers and Illustrators. Thanks go out to Lin Oliver, Jane Yolen, Dan Santat, Paul Zelinsky, Linda Bernfeld, Gaby Triana, Curtis Sponslor, Shannon Hitchcock, Augusta Scattergood, Heidi Stemple, Rob Sanders, Frank Remkiewicz, Janine Mason, Kerry Cerra, Hazel Mitchell, Debbi Ohi, Russ Cox, Sheri Barnes, Steve Asbell, Gladys Jose, and everyone else who makes this organization successful.

Thanks to my critique group, including Sara Pennypacker, Dianne Ochiltree, Toni Buzzeo, and Linda Shute, for offering invaluable advice and encouragement. Thank you, Dr. Kate L. Laskowski, for Skyping with me about spiders' social behaviors. Thank you, Joyce Sweeney, for the many fantastic writing workshops. Thank you, Lorin Oberweger and Donald Maass, for the brilliant Breakout Novel Intensive where *Garbage Island* came together.

Thank you, Tracey Adams of Adams Literary, for orchestrating the perfect partnership with amazing editor Rebecca Davis at Boyds Mills Press. You have both experienced me at my most insufferable moments, and I formally apologize for all past and future offenses. Thank you to the rest of the Boyds Mills team, including Liz, Brittany, Suzy, Cherie, Barbara, Tim, Toni, Sue, Kerry, and Michael.

Thank you, God, for turning the garbage of my life into a vessel that can serve a purpose. Thank you to Abby and Jack, who I love more than all the toilet paper in the world. And to the girl who writes fairy tales—the best is yet to come.